"I don't understand—"

"I imagine you're in shock." Joaquin closed a domineering hand over her shoulder, and urged her into the dim depths of the interior. It was obvious that the little house had stood empty for some time. "You thought you had got away scot-free with your confidence tricks. In fact, you believed you were about to enrich yourself again at Fidelio's expense—"

"I don't know what you're talking about!" Lucy protested.

"Then listen and you will find out," Joaquin advised very softly. "I took it upon myself to bring you here, and here you will stay for as long as I choose to keep you."

LYNNE GRAHAM was born in Northern Ireland and has been a keen Harlequin reader since her teens. She is very happily married to an understanding husband, who has learned to cook since she started to write! Her five children keep her on her toes. She has a very large Old English sheepdog, which knocks everything over, and two cats. When time allows, Lynne is a keen gardener.

Calling all Lynne Graham fans!

Lynne's next book will be available in November.
The Sicilian's Mistress
(Harlequin Presents® #2139)
is part of our heart-stopping AMNESIA series.

After three long years, Gianni D'Angelo has found Milly! However, she doesn't remember him. All she knows is that she was found after a hit-and-run accident, pregnant and with her memory gone.

Milly is horrified when she learns that she was Gianni's mistress...and now he's claiming that her little boy is his son! Gianni wants Milly back and wants to be a father to Connor, and his solution is simple: marriage!

Lynne Graham
DON JOAQUIN'S PRIDE

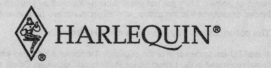

TORONTO • NEW YORK • LONDON
AMSTERDAM • PARIS • SYDNEY • HAMBURG
STOCKHOLM • ATHENS • TOKYO • MILAN • MADRID
PRAGUE • WARSAW • BUDAPEST • AUCKLAND

ISBN 0-373-12127-X

DON JOAQUIN'S PRIDE

First North American Publication 2000.

'I COULDN'T possibly pretend to be you...' Lucy's shaken voice trailed away, her incredulity unhidden.

'Why not?' Cindy demanded sharply. 'Guatemala is half a world away and Fidelio Paez has never met me. He doesn't even know I *have* a sister, never mind an identical twin!'

'But why can't you just write back and explain that you're not in a position to visit right now?' Lucy asked uneasily, struggling to understand why her sister should have suggested such an outrageous masquerade in response to a mere invitation, and why on earth she was getting so worked up about the matter.

'I wish it was that simple!'

'You're getting married in a month,' Lucy reminded her soothingly. 'As I see it, that makes a tactful refusal *very* simple.'

'You don't understand. It wasn't even Fidelio who wrote to me. It was some neighbour of his, some wretched interfering man called Del Castillo!' Cindy's beautifully manicured hands knotted together in a strained gesture, her full mouth tightening. 'He's demanding that I come over and stay for a while—'

'What business is it of his to demand anything?'

Cindy gave her an almost hunted look. 'He thinks that as Fidelio's daughter-in-law, his only surviving relative... well, that I owe the old boy a visit.'

'Why?' In other circumstances Lucy would have understood the demand, but it seemed rather excessive when seen

5

in the light of her twin's short-lived first marriage five years earlier.

While working in Los Angeles, Cindy had enjoyed a whirlwind romance with the son of a wealthy Guatemalan rancher. However, her sister had been widowed within days of becoming a bride. Although a young and apparently healthy man, Mario Paez had died of a sudden heart attack. At the time, Guatemala had been suffering severe floods. The whole country had been in uproar, with the communications system seriously disrupted. With what little she had known about her late husband's background, Cindy had found it impossible to get in touch with Mario's father in time for the funeral, so it had gone ahead without the older man and afterwards Cindy had flown straight back home to London.

'You know, you never even mentioned that you still kept in touch with Mario's father,' Lucy admitted, her violet-blue eyes warm with approval.

High spots of colour lit Cindy's taut cheekbones. 'I thought keeping in touch was the least I could do, and now that Fidelio's sick—'

'The old man's ill?' Lucy interrupted in dismay. 'Is it serious?'

'Yes. So how can I write back and say that I can't visit a dying man because I'm getting married again?'

Lucy winced. That would indeed be a most unfeeling response. In fact, from Fidelio's point of view it would only serve as a horribly cruel reminder of the tragically premature death of his only son.

'That man, that neighbour of his, has actually sent me plane tickets! But even if I wasn't getting married to Roger I wouldn't want to go,' Cindy confessed in a sudden raw rush of resentment. 'I *hate* sick people! I can't bear to be around them. I would be totally useless at being sympathetic and all that sort of stuff!'

Lowering her gaze, Lucy suppressed a sigh, unhappily aware that her twin was telling the truth. When their mother had become an invalid, Cindy had been hopeless. On the other hand, her sister's financial help had eased the more practical problems of those long difficult months when she herself had been forced to give up work to nurse their mother. Cindy had bought them a small apartment close to the hospital where their parent had been receiving treatment. Right now that apartment was back on the market; Lucy was keen to repay her sister's generosity.

'But you could easily cope with Fidelio,' Cindy pointed out, her eagerness to persuade her twin to take her place unhidden. 'You were absolutely marvellous with Mum. Florence Nightingale to the life!'

'But it wouldn't be right to deceive Fidelio Paez like that,' Lucy interposed uncomfortably. 'I think you should discuss this with Roger—'

'Roger?' Cindy froze at that reference to the man she adored and was soon to marry. 'He's the very last person I want to know about this!' Crossing the room, she reached for her sister's hands, a pleading look in her eyes. 'If Roger knew how much I owe Fidelio he would probably think that we should cancel the wedding so that I could go over there…and I couldn't *bear* that!'

Lucy stared back at her twin in bewilderment. 'What do you *owe* Fidelio Paez?'

'Over the years, he's…well, he's sent me a lot of money,' Cindy admitted with visible discomfiture.

Lucy's brows pleated, for her sister lived in some comfort and had never to her knowledge been short of cash in recent years. 'Why would Mario's father have sent you money?'

'Well, why shouldn't he have?' Cindy demanded almost aggressively. 'He's loaded, and he's got nobody else to spend it on. I got nothing when Mario died!'

Lucy flushed at her twin's frank annoyance over that reality.

Cindy's taut shoulders bowed then, and she breathed in deep. 'Yet in spite of all Fidelio's invitations I never visited him, and when he tried to arrange a date to come over here to meet me a couple of years back, I made excuses.'

Lucy was shocked by that confession. 'For goodness' sake, why?'

Cindy grimaced and shrugged. 'I haven't always been the world's nicest person, like *you* are, Lucy!' she muttered irritably, wiping away the tears in her eyes with an infuriated hand. 'Why would I want to go and stay on some ranch in the back of beyond with an old man? And why would I have wanted to be landed with entertaining him here in London? I always had something better to do, but I did *intend* to meet him sooner or later...only right *now* happens to be lousy timing!'

'Yes.' Lucy could see that, and no longer wondered why her sister's conscience was troubling her so much.

'Roger knows nothing about Fidelio, and I wouldn't like him to know about the money because he wouldn't think very much of me for just taking and taking and never giving anything back,' Cindy confided grudgingly, biting at her lip, her eyes filling with tears again. 'There's a lot that Roger doesn't know about my past, Lucy. I've put it behind me. I've changed. I made a new start when I got back in touch with you and Mum last year, and I haven't taken a penny from Fidelio since then—'

'It's all right,' Lucy muttered, her own eyes smarting at her twin's desperation and her uncharacteristic honesty.

'It *will* be if you go to Guatemala for me. I know I'm asking a lot, especially when I haven't exactly been honest about some things,' Cindy continued tautly. 'But I really do need your help with this, Lucy...and if you can do this *one* thing for me, I swear I'll be your best friend for ever!'

'Cindy, I—' Enveloped in a huge, grateful hug, Lucy was touched to the heart, because her sister was rarely demonstrative.

The twins had been separated by their divorcing parents at the age of seven and had spent the following fifteen years apart. Only recently had Lucy had the chance to get to know her sister again, and that had not been an easy task. Until now Cindy had hidden behind a reserve foreign to Lucy's more open nature, and their lifestyles and interests were so different that it had been a challenge to find shared ground on which to bridge those years of estrangement.

But now, for the first time since they were children, Cindy had confided in Lucy again and asked for her help. The idea that she could be needed by her infinitely more glamorous and successful sister astonished Lucy, but it made her feel proud as well. Once the quieter, more dependent twin, Lucy had been devastated when her bossier, livelier sister had disappeared from her life. She had never lost that inner ache of loneliness and loss, and Cindy's appeal for her help, Cindy's *need* for her, touched a deep chord of sympathy within her. Blocking out the more practical misgivings threatening at the back of her mind, Lucy smiled with determined eagerness to offer all the assistance within her power.

Cindy drew back and surveyed her twin with the critical eye of a woman who had worked as both a make-up artist and a fashion buyer and who took a great deal of interest in her own appearance.

Ironically, few identical twins could have looked more different. Lucy never used make-up and tied her defiantly curly caramel-blonde hair back at the nape of her neck. Her blue denim skirt was calf-length, her check shirt sensible and her shoes flat and comfortable.

'I sent Fidelio a photo of me last year and I was dressed

to kill. I'm going to have my work cut out turning *you* into *me*!' Cindy confessed with a rueful groan.

Lucy just stood there, slightly dazed, suddenly not quite sure she could have agreed to do such an outrageous thing as pretend to be her sister instead of herself. Her *homely* self. Now that they were both adults, she simply couldn't imagine looking like her twin. Cindy had the perfect grooming of a model and confidently revealed far more than she concealed of her slim, toned figure. Her blonde mane of hair hung in a smooth fall down her back, both straightened and lightened. Not one inch of Cindy was less than perfect, Lucy conceded, hurriedly curving her bitten nails into the centre of her palms and sucking in her stomach.

Outside the shabby bar, which was little more than a shack with a tin roof, a wizened little man in a poncho tied up his horse to the roadside post available and stomped in out of the sweltering heat. He joined the tough-looking cowboys standing by the bar and within ten seconds he was gaping at Lucy with the rest of them. In a badly creased pale pink designer suit and precarious high heels, she was a sight such as was rarely seen at this remote outpost in the Guatemalan Petén.

The humidity was horrendous. Pressing a crumpled tissue to her perspiring brow, Lucy studied the scarred table in mute physical misery. Cindy had insisted that she would need to dress to impress throughout her stay. But Lucy felt horribly uncomfortable and conspicuous in her borrowed finery. Furthermore the wretched shoes pinched her toes and nipped her heels like instruments of torture.

Yesterday she had flown into Guatemala City and connected with a domestic flight to Flores, where she had spent the night at a small hotel. She had expected to be taken from there to the Paez ranch, but instead she had been greeted with the message that she would be picked up at the crossroads at San Angelita. Once her ancient rattling cab had turned off the main highway the landscape had become steadily more arid, and the road had swiftly declined into a rutted dirt track. That incredibly long and dusty journey had finally brought her to a ramshackle little cluster of almost entirely abandoned buildings in the middle of a dustbowl overshadowed by what looked very much like a volcano and, according to her guidebook, probably was. Exhaustion and a deep, desperate desire for a bath now gripped Lucy, not to mention an increasingly strong attack of cold feet.

Suppose Fidelio realised that she *wasn't* Cindy? Suppose she said or did something that exposed their deception? It would be simply appalling if her masquerade was uncovered. A sick old man certainly didn't require any further distress. But what would have been the alternative? Lucy asked herself unhappily. Cindy wouldn't have come, and the thought of Fidelio Paez passing away without a single relative to comfort him filled Lucy with helpless compassion.

Belatedly registering that the noisy clump of men at the bar had fallen silent, Lucy looked up. A very tall male, who looked as if he had walked straight out of a spaghetti western in the role of cold-blooded *killer*, now stood just inside the doorway, spurred and booted feet set slightly astride. Intimidated by one glittering glance from beneath the dusty brim of the black hat that shadowed his lean, hard-boned features, Lucy gulped and hurriedly endeavoured to curl her five foot tall body into an even less noticeable hunch behind the table.

The barman surged out from behind the counter and extended a moisture-beaded glass to the new arrival. A doffing of hats and a low murmur of respectful greeting broke the silence. Emptying it in a long, thirsty gulp, the man handed the glass back and sauntered with disturbing cat-like fluidity and jingling spurs across to the far corner where Lucy sat.

'Lucinda Paez?' he drawled.

Lucy focused wide-eyed on the leather belt with gleaming silver inserts that encircled his lean hips. Then, not liking the menacing manner in which he was towering over her, she thrust her chair back and hurriedly scrambled upright. Even in her four-inch heels, it didn't help much. He had dwarfed the other men at the bar. He had to be six foot three, and the crown of her head barely reached his shoulder. Wondering if she was going to need her Spanish phrase book to make herself understood, she gazed up at his aggressive jawline and swallowed hard. 'You're here to collect me?' she queried weakly. 'I didn't hear a car.'

'That could be because I arrived on a horse.'

For a split second his smooth grasp of colloquial English took her by surprise, and then an uneasy laugh escaped her. He could only be cracking a joke. You didn't turn up on horseback to collect a person with luggage. Tilting her golden head back, and fighting her natural shyness with all her might, Lucy said apologetically, 'Could you show me some identification, please?'

'I'm afraid I have none to offer. I am Joaquin Francisco Del Castillo, and I am not accustomed to doubt on that point.'

Lucy tried and failed to swallow on that staggeringly arrogant assurance. He had thrown his head high as if she had insulted him, his strong jawline rigid. 'Well, Señor...er...Del Castillo, I am not accustomed to going off with strange men—'

'*Es verdad?* You picked up Mario in a Los Angeles bar and shared his bed the same night. That knowledge does not lead me to believe that you are a particularly cautious woman,' he drawled, his growling accent roughening the vowel sounds.

Lucy was nailed to the spot, still focusing on that firm male beautifully modelled mouth. She blinked, her soft lips opening and closing again in shock. She just could not *believe* that he had said something so offensive right to her face. Burning colour slowly crawled up her throat. 'How dare you?' she whispered in a shaken undertone. 'That is a complete untruth!'

'Mario and I grew up together. You are wasting your time putting on an act for my benefit. Save it for Fidelio. Are you coming…or are you staying here?'

'I'm not going any place with you! They can send some-one else out from the ranch,' Lucy informed him with re-straint, from between clenched teeth.

'There *is* no one else, *señora*.' And, with that clipped retort, Joaquin Del Castillo simply turned on his heel and strode back outside, command and cool writ large in his straight back, wide shoulders and fluid measured carriage.

Still awash with sheer paralysed shock at being treated with so shattering a lack of respect, Lucy stayed where she was. The men at the bar were talking between themselves. She stole a cringing glance at the growing male huddle, appalled by the suspicion that one of them might have un-derstood enough English to follow what Joaquin Del Castillo had slung at her. Her cheeks aflame with colour, she grabbed up her heavy suitcase and struggled back out-side with it.

Joaquin Del Castillo was waiting for her.

'You are the most rude, foul-mouthed man I have ever met,' Lucy announced, giving him only the most minimal sidewise glance of acknowledgement. 'Please do not speak to me again unless it is absolutely necessary.'

'You can't bring that case.' Before she could even guess

his intention he had swept it up in one lean brown hand, planted it down in the dust and sprung it open.

'What are you doing?' Lucy gasped, her frigid air of desperate dignity fracturing fast.

'It's a long ride and I want to make good time. You will have no need for all these fripperies on the ranch,' Joaquin Del Castillo asserted grimly. 'Pick out a few necessities and I'll put them in the saddlebags. The bar owner will look after your case until you return.'

'A long ride…?' Lucy repeated weakly. 'Are you seriously expecting me…to get on a horse?'

'Fidelio sold his pick-up.'

'A h-horse?' Lucy said again, even more shakily.

'In a few hours it will be getting dark. I suggest you go behind the bar and change into a more appropriate outfit for the journey.'

Fidelio had sold his pick-up? Certainly a seriously ill old man would have little need of personal transport. But Fidelio Paez was also a wealthy man, and Lucy would have thought that any big ranch needed at least one vehicle. But what did she know about ranching? she asked herself, ruefully conceding her abysmal ignorance on the subject. Evidently Joaquin Del Castillo didn't have motorised transport either, and she had seen for herself how poor and few were the roads in the Petén.

Lucy snatched in a deep shuddering breath. She had never been on a horse's back in her life. 'I can't ride…'

A broad muscular shoulder sheathed in fine black cotton shrugged. It was fluid, it was dismissive, it was impatient. In fact Joaquin Del Castillo had the kind of highly expressive body language that made speech quite unnecessary. With the heel of one lean brown hand he pushed back the brim of his hat and surveyed her without pity. Sunlight illuminated his lean dark features for the first time.

Lucy's breath tripped in her throat. He was so incredibly

handsome she just stared and kept on staring, involuntary fascination gripping her.

His eyes were a clear startling green, framed by spiky ebony lashes and shockingly unexpected in that bold sun-bronzed face. His high, proud cheekbones were dissected by a lean, arrogant blade of a nose, the brilliant eyes crowned by flaring black brows, the whole brought to vibrant life by a mouth as passionate and as wicked as sin. He was just so gorgeous she was transfixed to the spot.

Their eyes met. An infinitesimal little tremor ran through Lucy. Her heart skipped a beat, began thundering in her ears instead. Green like emeralds, green like fire. A thought which didn't make any sense at all, but then nothing that Lucy experienced in that moment had anything to do with normal thought. She watched the colour score his fabulous cheekbones with a level of wonderment that was undeniably mindless. Insidious heat curled up in the pit of her stomach, making her suck in her breath and blink, and at the same moment she blinked *he* turned away.

Sudden appalled embarrassment engulfed Lucy as she realised how she had been behaving. She was supposed to be choosing clothes from her case. What on earth had she been doing, gaping at him like some starstruck schoolgirl? Mortified by her own adolescent behaviour, Lucy crouched down beside her case and struggled to concentrate. 'I can't ride,' she muttered afresh.

'The mare is quiet.' His rich, dark drawl had a disturbingly rough edge.

Her hands were trembling as she rooted clumsily through all the designer clothing which her twin had given her on loan. *He* was standing there watching her, and every time she turned up a piece of lingerie she blushed furiously and thrust it hurriedly back out of sight. He looked like a film star but he had the manners of a pig. But then he probably didn't know any better, born and bred in the back of be-

yond, surrounded by a lot of cattle and grass, she told herself bracingly. She pulled out a pair of pale blue stretch
cotton pedal pushers and an embroidered gypsy top, neither
of which she fancied wearing—but unfortunately they were
the only remotely casual garments which Cindy had been
prepared to include.

'I can't get changed without privacy,' she told Joaquin
tautly.

'You're not modest…why pretend? Not two months after
Mario died you were flashing everything you've got in a
men's magazine centrefold!'

Lucy closed stricken eyes in horror and chagrin. She
knew so little about her twin's life during the years they
had been apart. And this hateful, dreadful man seemed to
be revelling in making offensive allegations. How did he
know so much about Cindy? *Had* her sister met Mario in
a bar and slept with him the very same night? Lucy cringed,
knowing she was a real prude but unable to stifle her shame
on her sister's behalf. *Had* Cindy engaged in nude model-
ling before she'd decided to train as a make-up artist?

But then stripping off for the camera was not the shocking choice it had once been, Lucy reminded herself bracingly. Famous actresses did it now, proud and unashamed
of their beautiful bodies. Adam and Eve had been unclothed
and unashamed too, until the serpent got at them. How
dared this crude backwoods rancher sneer at her twin?

'I believe I asked you only to address me again if it was
unavoidable,' Lucy reminded him in the same icy tone she
would have used to quell a very badly behaved child in the
library where she had once worked.

Behind the bar, which rejoiced in nothing as sophisticated as a window on the back wall, she kicked off her
shoes and peeled off her tights at frantic speed, and then
hauled up the clinging pedal-pushers beneath her skirt. By
the time she reappeared her elaborately teased mane of

carefully coiffed hair, which she had refused to have straightened or tinted, was flopping into a wild torrent of damp ringlets, and the nape of her neck, the slope of her breasts and her face were wet with perspiration.

Joaquin Del Castillo then subjected Lucy to the kind of long, slow scrutiny she was wholly unused to receiving from his sex. But Cindy enjoyed attracting male attention and chose her wardrobe accordingly. So the pedal-pushers were a tight fit, chosen to accentuate the lush female curve of hip and thigh, and the cropped gypsy top was thin and low-cut. Lacking her sister's confidence, however, Lucy was plunged by that insolent male appraisal into instant red-hot discomfiture.

The silence seemed to go on and on and on. Her cheeks burned. She was conscious of her body in a way she had never been conscious of it before. Her breasts felt oddly full and heavy, stirring with the increased rapidity of her breathing. He looked, and she...*and she*? She couldn't think straight.

Joaquin Del Castillo veiled his gaze.

In bewilderment, Lucy lowered her own gaze, dismayed by the accelerated thump of her own heartbeat, the shortness of her breath, that lingering sense of being dislocated from time. She frowned at the space where she had left her case earlier and muttered unevenly, 'Where's my case?'

Without the slightest warning, Joaquin strode forward and dropped a rough wool poncho over her shoulders, engulfing her in yards of scratchy malodorous fabric. 'What on earth are you doing?' she cried, pulling at the garment with distaste.

Impervious to her reaction, Joaquin Del Castillo planted a battered straw hat on her head. 'Treat the sun with respect or you will burn your skin to a withered crisp!'

'Where's my case?' Lucy demanded afresh.

'I packed for you. Come on. We have no more time to waste.'

'You went through my personal things?' Lucy was aghast at the idea of a man rustling through her panties and her bras.

'Let's go,' he grated impatiently.

For some reason there was a general exodus from the bar at the same moment. The cowboy horde poured out through the door to watch Joaquin prod a deeply reluctant Lucy round to the side of the sleek brown mare tethered to the rail.

'You grasp the rein, place your left foot in the stirrup and then you swing yourself up into the saddle,' he instructed smoothly.

Lucy's teeth gritted. She could hear suppressed male laughter behind her. Planting a canvas-shod foot into the stirrup cup, she hauled herself up by dint of sheer determination, but she didn't raise her other leg quite high enough and simultaneously the mare changed position. Unbalanced, Lucy fell back hard on her bottom and snaked her flailing legs back in fright as the mare's hooves skittered too close for comfort.

A powerful hand closed over hers and hauled her upright again with stunning ease. 'Would you like some help, *señora*?'

Sardonic amusement was audible in that honeyed dark drawl. A tide of unfamiliar rage drew Lucy's every muscle taut. She snatched her fingers free of his patronising hold. 'I'd have managed if the blasted horse hadn't moved!' she told him with furious resentment. 'And I'll do it without your help if it kills me…so stand back and snigger with your friends, because it's obvious that that's all that you're good for!'

A line of dark colour highlighted his amazing cheek-

bones. Then that expressive mouth set like moulded steel.
'As you wish...but I would not like to see you injured.'

'Get out of my way!' Lucy snarled, a tiny proportion of
her brain standing back in disbelief at her own fiery behaviour.

Grasping the rein afresh, Lucy was now powered by so
much temper she could have swung up high enough to
touch the sun. Seconds later, she found herself surveying
the ground from an elevated position. Squaring her slight
shoulders, she tried to ease her right foot into the other
stirrup. But it was done for her. Long cool fingers clasped
her ankle and provided guidance. Lucy was in no way mol-
lified by that belated piece of assistance, but she said thank
you in a cold little voice just to show that she had been
better brought up than he had been.

'I will attach a leading rein to the mare. You will not be
in any danger,' Joaquin Del Castillo asserted with a chilling
lack of expression.

Briefly her forehead indented. He sounded for all the
world like a drawling, icily self-contained aristocrat de-
pressing the rude pretensions of a member of the lower
orders. She shook her head at that foolish false impression.

Obviously her outburst had offended him. Good, she told
herself. He had been asking for it. Boy, had he been asking
for a metaphoric slap in the face in front of their now silent
audience! Nobody was smirking or sniggering now; she
might feel somewhat shaken by the experience of having
shouted at someone for the first time in her life, but in the
aftermath she was *proud* of herself. And then the living,
breathing animal beneath her rigid hips shifted with
alarming effect.

'*Joaquin...?*' Lucy whispered with sick but definite emphasis. 'The horse is m-moving again.'

'Try not to stiffen up. It will make Chica nervous,' he

responded in a curiously constrained tone as he bent his head.

'Do you think I'm not nervous, stuck up here ten feet off the ground?' Lucy gasped before she could snatch the words back.

He spread fluid hands very slowly and stepped back. 'I assure you that you will come to no harm.'

In strained silence, she watched him attach what he had called a leading rein to the huge black stallion twitching its hooves like a threatening volcano several feet away. 'I hope you can control that monster...I hope it's not going to run away with you—'

'No horse has ever run away with me, *señora*,' Joaquin Del Castillo gritted, half under his breath.

And if any had he certainly wouldn't admit it, Lucy decided. Joaquin Del Castillo was of a breed of male utterly unknown to her. All sizzling, musclebound temperament and just bursting with pride over the fact. Any form of weakness, she sensed, would be anathema to him. And he despised her...well, he despised Cindy, and, as she was pretending to *be* Cindy, she was stuck with being despised.

But why was Joaquin Del Castillo being so hostile and rude? After all, she had dutifully come to visit Fidelio, as he had demanded. And, whether he knew it or not, he could thank his lucky stars that she *wasn't* Cindy. Her twin would have been halfway back to the airport by now! Cindy had a very quick temper, not to mention a love and expectation of comfort. Furthermore, accustomed as she was to male admiration, Cindy would never have withstood the attacks and indignities meted out to the sister eleven minutes her junior.

Ironically, Cindy had forecast that Lucy would be treated like a princess from the moment she arrived in Guatemala. Apparently Fidelio Paez's letters had shown him to be an old-fashioned gentleman with an instinctive need to be protective towards any member of the female sex. But Fidelio was generations older than his neighbour, Joaquin Del Castillo, Lucy conceded wryly. There was no intrinsic old-world Latin gallantry to be had from her companion. Why? Evidently he saw Cindy as a scarlet woman just because she had slept with Mario on their first date. What did he think a whirlwind romance entailed? So Cindy had got carried away by love and passion. How dared he sneer?

'How is Fidelio?' Lucy suddenly asked.

Joaquin shot her a grim glance. 'You finally remembered him?'

Lucy flushed.

'He is as well as can be expected in the circumstances.' With that scathing and uninformative assurance, he leapt up into the saddle and made further enquiry impossible.

As the horses plodded at a snail's pace out of the tiny settlement, Lucy focused on his wide-shouldered back view. Joaquin Del Castillo moved as if he was part of the stallion. Lucy endeavoured to unknot her own tense muscles, but she was so terrified of falling off that no sooner did she contrive to loosen one muscle than two others tightened in compensation.

'Slow down!' she called frantically within minutes, when the pace speeded up and her hips started to rise and fall bruisingly on the hard saddle beneath her.

He reined in and swung round. 'What's wrong?'

'If I fall off and break a leg, I won't be much use to Fidelio!' Lucy warned, with a strained attempt at an apologetic smile.

'Soon it will be dark—'

'So you keep on promising,' Lucy muttered limply, convinced she was boiling alive beneath her poncho. 'I can hardly wait for that sun to sink.'

'I am so sorry that this means of travel is not to your taste, señora.'

'Oh, call me Lucy, for goodness' sake. That formal address is a nonsense when you match it with your appalling
manners!'

Before her eyes Joaquin Del Castillo froze, hard jawline
squaring, nostrils flaring.

'I do realise that you neither like nor approve of me, and
I can't stand hypocrisy,' Lucy admitted uncomfortably, her
voice dying away in the stillness of his complete silence.

'Your name is Cindy. Why would I call you Lucy?'

In horror at her accidental slip, Lucy bent her head, suddenly belatedly grateful that her late parents had seen fit to
name their twin daughters Lucinda and Lucille. 'Most people call me Lucy now. Cindy was for the teen years,' she
lied breathlessly.

'Lucinda,' he sounded out with syllabic thoroughness,
and pressed his knees into the stallion's flanks.

Lucy struggled to stay on board the mare as they wended
their way out across the bleached grass plain. The empti-
ness was eerie. Sky and grass, and all around the heat, like
a hard physical entity beating down on her without remorse.
There were no buildings, no people, not even the cattle she
had dimly expected to see. The eventual sight of a gnarled
set of palm trees on a very slight incline should have been
enough for her to throw her hat high in celebration. But
she didn't have enough energy left. Indeed, by that stage
she had already lost all track of time. Even to shrug back
the poncho, lift one wrist and glance at her watch felt like
too much effort.

'I need a drink,' she finally croaked, her mouth dry as a
bone.

'There is a water bottle attached to your saddle,' Joaquin
informed her drily over his shoulder. 'But don't drink too
much. You'll make yourself sick.'

'You'll have to get the bottle,' Lucy told him in a small
voice, because really she was beginning to feel like the

biggest whiniest drag in the whole of Guatemala. 'I don't like looking down. It makes me feel dizzy.'

Joaquin Del Castillo rode the stallion round in a circle, leant out across the divide between their respective mounts with acrobatic confidence and detached the water bottle, the fluid movement simplistic in its highly deceptive air of effortless ease. Indeed, the whole operation took Lucy's breath away.

'I saw a Cossack rider do something like that at a circus once,' Lucy confided shyly.

'I did not learn to ride in a circus, *señora*,' Joaquin Del Castillo responded with icy hauteur.

'It was meant to be a compliment, actually.' Turning her discomfited face away, Lucy let the water drift down into her parched mouth.

'That's enough,' Joaquin Del Castillo told her within seconds.

Lucy handed the bottle back, wiped her mouth with an unsteady hand and drooped like a dying swan over Chica's silky mane. With a groaned imprecation in Spanish, Joaquin Del Castillo sprang out of the saddle and planted his hands on her waist. 'Let go of the reins.'

In surprise, Lucy unclenched her stiff fingers and found herself swept down from the mare into a pair of frighteningly powerful arms. 'What on earth—?'

'You will ride with me on El Lobo,' Joaquin announced as he swung her up on to the huge stallion's back, following her up so fast into the saddle she didn't even have the chance to argue.

As Lucy curved uneasily away from the hard heat of his lean, muscular thighs, a strong arm settled round her abdomen and forced her inexorably back. 'Stay still...I will not allow you to fall,' he said impatiently.

Shaken by the sudden intimate contact of their bodies, Lucy dragged in a deep, shivering breath. The disturbingly

insidious scent of warm male assailed her. Her dry mouth
ran even dryer. He smelt of hot skin and horse. Something
twisted low in her tummy, increasing her nervous unease,
but at least she felt safe in his hold. As her tension ebbed,
slow, pervasive warmth blossomed in its stead, making her
feel strangely limp and yielding. The soft peaks of her
breasts tightened into hard little points, filling her with a
heat that had nothing to do with the relentless sun above.
She jerked taut on the shattering acknowledgement that her
body was responding without her volition to the sexually
charged sizzle of Joaquin Del Castillo's raw masculinity.

'Relax,' he murmured softly, long brown fingers splaying
across her midriff to ease her back into position again.

When he talked, soft and low, he had the most beautiful
dark honeyed accent, she thought abstractedly, and never
had she been as outrageously aware of anything as she was
of that lean hand pressing just below her breasts. Her heart
was pounding like a hammer inside her ribcage.

'You're holding me too tightly,' she complained uneasily, horrified and embarrassed by the effect he was having
on her.

'You are not in any danger,' Joaquin Del Castillo
drawled silkily above her head. 'I am not attracted by
stunted women with bleached hair and streaky fake tans.'

A lump ballooned in Lucy's convulsed throat. Mortified
pink chased away her strained pallor. 'You really are the
most loathsome man,' she gasped. 'And I can't wait to see
the back of you! When will we reach Fidelio's ranch?'

'Tomorrow—'

'*Tomorrow?*' Lucy croaked in stunned disbelief.

'In an hour, we will make camp for the night.'

Camp…*camp*? Aghast at the prospect of spending the
night outdoors, Lucy swallowed back a self-pitying moan
with the greatest of difficulty. 'I thought we would be arriving soon—'

'We have not made good time, *señora*.'

'I had no idea that the ranch was so far away,' she confided miserably.

They rode on in silence, and slowly the sun became a fiery orb in its sliding path towards the horizon. Lucy was by then dazed with exhaustion and half asleep. She was plucked from the stallion's back and set down on solid earth again, but her legs had all the strength of bending twigs. She staggered, aching in bone and muscle from neck to toe. Dimly she focused on a trio of gnarled palm trees silhouetted against the darkening night sky and experienced a vague sense of *déjà vu*. But they couldn't possibly be the same trees she had noticed hours back! No doubt one set of palm trees looked much like another, Lucy conceded wearily, and she definitely couldn't recall the slender ribbon of river she could now see running nearby.

With every step she cursed her own bodily weakness. She had lost a lot of weight while her mother had been ill, and only the previous month had come down with a nasty bout of flu. After two solid days of travelling she had no energy left, and was indeed feeling far from well. It had not occurred to either her or Cindy that Fidelio's ranch might lie in such a remote and inaccessible location.

The Guatemalan lowlands had looked infinitely less vast and daunting on the map than they were in reality, and, torn from the familiarity of city life and her own careful routine, Lucy felt horrendously vulnerable. Her twin might have travelled the globe but this was Lucy's first trip abroad. Freedom had been the one thing her adoring but possessive mother had refused to give her.

Joaquin was seeing to the horses by the river when Lucy returned. She saw him through a haze of utter exhaustion. Her legs were trembling beneath her. She sank down on the grass. He dropped a blanket beside her.

'You must be hungry,' he murmured.

Lucy shook her head, too sick with fatigue to feel hunger. Slowly, like a toy running out of battery power, she slumped down full length. 'Sleepy,' she mumbled thickly.

Surprising her once again, he spread the blanket for her. Then, bending down, he shook her even more by sweeping her up in one easy motion and laying her down on the blanket. 'Rest, then,' he drawled flatly.

Joaquin Del Castillo was a male of innate and fascinating contradictions, Lucy acknowledged sleepily. Fiercely proud and icily self-contained in his hostility towards her, yet too honourable, it seemed, to make her suffer unnecessary discomfort.

Against the backdrop of the flaming sunset, he stood over her like a huge black intimidating shadow. 'You look like the devil,' she whispered, with a drowsy attempt at humour.

'I will not take your soul, *señora*...but I have every intention of stripping you of everything else you possess.'

Stray words fluttered in the blankness of Lucy's brain. They did not connect. They did not make sense. With a soundless sigh of relief, Lucy sank into the deep, dreamless sleep of exhaustion.

CHAPTER TWO

LUCY opened her eyes slowly.

A small fire was crackling, sending out shooting sparks.
No wonder she had awakened, she thought in astonishment.
The night was warm and humid, yet Joaquin Del Castillo
was subjecting her to the heat of a fire. She scrambled back
from it, her eyes adjusting only gradually to his big dark
silhouette on the other side of the leaping flames.

Pushing a self-conscious hand through her tangled curls,
Lucy sat up just as a hair-raising cry sounded from somewhere out in the darkness. Lucy flinched, her head jerking
as she glanced fearfully over her shoulder.

'What was that?'

'Jaguar...they hunt at night.'

Lucy inched back closer to the fire and her companion
and shivered. He extended a tin cup of coffee and she
curved her unsteady hands round the cup and sipped grate-
fully, even though the pungent bitter brew contained neither
sugar nor milk. 'How soon tomorrow will we get to
Fidelio's ranch?' she pressed.

In the flickering light his strikingly handsome features
clenched, the lush crescent of his ebony lashes casting fan-
like shadows on his hard cheekbones. 'Early.'

'I suppose we would have got there tonight if I'd been
able to ride,' Lucy conceded, striving to proffer an olive
branch for the sake of peace. He might despise her, but she
was remembering the plane tickets he had sent at his own
expense. He didn't look as if he was terribly well off, yet
he had made a very generous gesture. Without doubt
Fidelio had a caring and concerned neighbour, willing to

27

go to a lot of trouble on his behalf. She might loathe
Joaquin Del Castillo, and every bone in her body might
feel battered by that almost unendurable ride, but she could
still respect the motives which had prompted him to demand that Cindy visit her father-in-law.

Joaquin shrugged a sleek, muscular broad shoulder and
passed her a plate.

Lucy surveyed the roughly sliced bread and cheese, and
a fruit she didn't even recognise, and then tucked in with
an appetite that surprised her.

Having cleared the plate, and drained the coffee in a final
appreciative gulp, she felt the continuing silence weigh
heavily on her. 'Perhaps you'll tell me now how Fidelio
really is,' she prompted, with a small uncertain smile of
encouragement.

'You will see the situation soon enough.'

His cool steady gaze and his sonorous accented drawl
had a curiously chilling quality. A faint spasm of alarm
crawled up Lucy's spine and raised gooseflesh on her arms.
But as quickly as she found herself reacting in fear, she
told herself off. Being brought up by a mother who hated
and distrusted all men had made her over-sensitive.

Lucy had been seven when her father met another
woman and demanded a divorce. Cindy, always his favourite, had become a real handful after he'd moved out.
Infuriated by her daughter's increasingly difficult behaviour, their mother had complained that it wasn't fair that
she should be left to raise both children alone. In the end
Peter and Jean Fabian had divided their twin daughters between them in much the same way that they had divided
their possessions.

Her father and Cindy had moved to Scotland, where her
father had set up a new business. He had promised that his
daughters would be able to exchange visits but it had never
happened. And, embittered by her husband's desertion for

the younger, prettier woman he had replaced her with, Jean Fabian had clung to the daughter who remained with feverish protectiveness. A rebound romance in which she had once again been betrayed and humiliated had set the seal on her mother's prejudices. Lucy's teenage years had been poisoned by her mother's hatred for the male sex. The endless restrictions she had endured had made it impossible for her to hang on to her friends.

By the time she had been ready to make a stand and demand a social life of her own Jean Fabian's health had been failing, and Lucy's imprisonment outside working hours had become complete. When she had tried to go out even occasionally she had been treated to sobbing hysterical accusations of selfish neglect and threats of suicide.

However, her poor sister had suffered infinitely more in their father's care, Lucy reminded herself, ashamed of her momentary pang of self-pity. Her mother *had* loved and looked after her. But when her father's new business had failed and his girlfriend had walked out on him, Peter Fabian had apparently degenerated into a surly drunk, forever in debt and unable to hold down a job. Cindy had been frank on the subject of her childhood experiences at least. Her sister had had a rough time. Indeed, listening to her talk, Lucy had felt horribly guilty about the security which she herself had taken for granted.

Tugging the blanket back round her again, Lucy lay down and stared up into a night sky studded with stars. She could cope with Joaquin Del Castillo's icy antagonism for another few hours. He didn't matter, she told herself. She was here for Fidelio's sake, and instead of feeling threatened by what was strange and different in Guatemala she should be seizing the opportunity to enjoy what she could of the experience.

Lucy was in agony when she tried to move the next morning. Her mistreated muscles had seized up and a night on the hard ground hadn't helped to ease her aching limbs. Sore all over, she accepted the small amount of water and the toilet bag which Joaquin silently offered her and removed herself to the comparative shelter of the palms to freshen up as best she could.

She could hardly walk. If anything, she felt worse than she had the night before, and the air was surprisingly cool. Shivering violently, she returned to the low-burning fire and donned the old poncho without being asked, grateful for its shielding warmth.

Joaquin passed her a cup of black coffee and more bread and cheese. He ate standing up, with the quick economical movements of an energetic male in a hurry.

As he helped her mount Chica Lucy gritted her teeth when her every muscle screeched in complaint. Another couple of hours at most, she told herself bracingly, but in no time at all the ride became yet another endurance test.

When the mare finally drifted to an unannounced halt, Lucy muttered, 'Why have we stopped?' sooner than go to the trouble of raising her aching head.

Joaquin lifted her down from the mare. For a split second she was in close contact with his lithe, superbly masculine body. The sun-warmed virile scent of him engulfed her. As he lowered her to the ground her breasts rubbed against the muscular wall of his chest. Her nipples pinched taut and throbbed and Lucy sucked in a dismayed breath, her face colouring with embarrassment.

A pair of lean hands curved over her stiff shoulders and carefully turned her round. Her already shaken eyes opened even wider in surprise. A dingy little house with stucco walls lay only a few yards away. Tumbledown out-housing and a broken line of ancient fencing accentuated its forlorn air of desertion and neglect.

'Where are we?' she whispered in bewilderment.

'This is Fidelio's ranch, *señora*.' Joaquin Del Castillo raked her stunned face with hard, glittering eyes. 'I do hope that you will enjoy your stay here.'

'This...*this* is Fidelio's ranch?' Lucy queried unevenly, staring with glazed fixity at the hovel before her.

'No doubt you were expecting a more luxurious dwelling...'

Inwardly, Lucy winced at his perception. Swift shame engulfed her. The old man was ill and alone and he had evidently come down in the world over the past five years. He had fallen on hard times, *very* hard times. Her compassionate heart bled for Fidelio, and now she understood exactly why Joaquin Del Castillo had thought it necessary to send those plane tickets. Clearly Cindy's father-in-law couldn't possibly have afforded such a gesture on his own behalf.

'I would suggest that this humble abode is a most unpleasant surprise to you, *señora*. We both know that you would not have troubled to make this journey had you not believed that it would be well worth your while to attend a dying man's bedside,' Joaquin Del Castillo drawled with freezing bite.

With a frown of confusion, her concentration running at a tenth of its usual efficiency, Lucy gazed blankly back at her dark brooding companion with his unnerving air of command and authority. He was towering over her like an executioner, and involuntarily she took a nervous step back from him. 'What are you talking about? Why aren't we going inside? I want to see Fidelio—'

Joaquin vented a harsh laugh of disbelief. 'Fortunately for him, he is not here.'

'Not here?' Lucy frowned. 'You mean he's been taken into hospital?'

'No. Only the sick go to hospital, and Fidelio is *not* sick.'

A wiry little man of Central American Indian ancestry

suddenly appeared out of the deep shade cast by the out-housing and cast Lucy into even greater confusion. 'Who's that, then?'

'Mateo works for me.'

With that assurance, Joaquin strode forward to greet his employee. A brief exchange of a language she didn't even recognise took place. Then the older man retreated back into the shadows again. Not once had he angled so much as a curious glance in Lucy's direction.

Returning to her side, Joaquin threw wide the battered door on the little stucco house. 'Fidelio is not on his death-bed,' he then informed her with grim satisfaction. 'He is currently working many miles from here and he has no idea that you are even *in* Guatemala.'

'I don't understand—'

'I imagine you're in shock.' Joaquin closed a domineering hand over her shoulder and urged her into the dim depths of the interior, which contained only a few pieces of dusty decrepit furniture. It was obvious that the little house had stood empty for some time. 'You thought you had got away scot-free with your confidence tricks. In fact you believed you were about to enrich yourself yet again at Fidelio's expense—'

'I don't know what you're talking about!' Lucy protested.

'Then listen and you will find out,' Joaquin advised very softly. 'I took it upon myself to bring you here, and here you will stay for as long as I choose to keep you.'

Pale with apprehension, her head reeling, Lucy felt her way clumsily down into a rough wooden chair before her legs gave way beneath her. 'Fidelio isn't here,' she recited in shaky repetition. 'And he's *not* ill…and you are saying that you plan to *keep* me here…what on earth are you try-ing to say?' She pressed a weak hand to her pounding tem-ples. 'I must have misunderstood you—'

'You have misunderstood nothing. But you are naturally reluctant to face the reality that the golden goose will lay no more eggs,' Joaquin intoned grimly. 'And that while your pathetic begging letters were sufficient to impress Fidelio, they left a very different impression on me!'

'Begging letters?' Lucy questioned, her brow indenting.

With a scorching glance of savage contempt, Joaquin Del Castillo swept up the small wooden box resting on the hearth. Opening it, he planted it down on the rickety table beside her. 'Your own letters, *señora*. In every single one of them you talk of your poverty, your terrible struggle to survive…your desperate need for financial help!'

Like a woman caught up in a bad dream, Lucy reached out an unsteady hand and lifted an envelope, instantly recognising her sister's distinctive handwriting. As she dropped the envelope again her stomach performed a sick somersault. Poverty…struggle to survive…*Cindy*? Cindy, who had inherited a large amount of money from their father in an insurance pay-out at nineteen? Cindy, who spent like there was no tomorrow and who only ever bought the very best?

'And yet throughout that entire period you were living in style and security,' Joaquin Del Castillo delivered with fierce condemnation.

'How do you know that?' Fathoms deep in shock at what she was being told, Lucy nonetheless struggled to concentrate.

'I had enquiries made in London. You own an expensive Docklands apartment and take regular trips abroad,' Joaquin derided with a curled lip. 'You have enjoyed a most lavish lifestyle at Fidelio's expense. You played on the chivalry and compassion of a trusting, unworldly old man and it has taken you only five years to fleece him of all his savings!'

'Oh, dear heaven...' Lucy mumbled in sick comprehension.

'Your constant demands for money ruined him. This *was* to have been Fidelio's retirement home,' Joaquin Del Castillo shot at her with harsh condemnation. 'Before you began dipping your hand deep into his pocket Fidelio had the means to transform this place and look forward to a comfortable retirement after a lifetime of hard work. But now, when he should be taking his ease in his old age, he has been forced to take another job just to support himself!'

'I thought that Fidelio was a wealthy man—'

'How could you think that a ranch foreman was wealthy, *señora*?' Joaquin demanded with crushing derision.

'A ranch *foreman*? I think there's been a t-terrible misunderstanding,' Lucy stammered, a look of growing horror in her strained eyes.

The Central American rancher dropped down into an athletic crouch and gripped the arms of her chair, making her feel cornered and trapped. Blistering green eyes glittered threat at her. 'Don't play stupid with me...I'm not a patient man. There has been no misunderstanding. Accept now that there will be no easy escape from your imprisonment—'

'Imprisonment?' Lucy yelped, already recoiling from his menacing proximity. 'For goodness' sake...are you threatening me?'

'Until such time as you choose to sign a legally binding agreement to repay the money you virtually stole from Fidelio you will remain here,' Joaquin Del Castillo decreed. 'But you are in no danger of suffering any form of violence. I would not soil my hands with you!'

'Is that supposed to be reassuring?' Lucy asked in a very wobbly voice, while she wondered what was wrong with her malfunctioning brain. For on one level she was jerking back from him like some prudish Victorian maiden, and on another level she was staring into those extraordinary green eyes of his and marvelling at their beauty.

'Do you dare to suggest that I would use physical force on a woman?' Joaquin demanded in outrage. 'I...a Del Castillo, stoop to so shameful an act?'

Dry-mouthed, Lucy simply gaped at him. Sizzling eyes the colour of jade were focused on her. All that passion, all that fire, concealed from her and rigorously suppressed throughout their journey. No wonder Joaquin Del Castillo hadn't been able to manage much in the way of casual conversation! His efforts to conceal that incredibly volatile temperament from her must have been as constraining as a gag.

He sprang fluidly upright again. His bold sun-bronzed features were hard as iron. 'Mateo remains outside, purely to ensure your safety. There is nothing around you here but mile after empty mile of cattle country. This is a most dangerous and inhospitable terrain for the inexperienced.'

'You can't *make* me stay here,' Lucy told him dazedly.

He swept up a folded document from the table and extended it. 'If you sign this, you may leave immediately. Without a signature, you remain.'

Lucy snatched the document from him. Mercifully it was written in English, but it was couched in long-winded legalese. Slowly and with a straining frown of effort she worked down the page, and then came to a sum of money that was so large it jolted her into even deeper shock. According to what she was reading, Cindy had received the most enormous sum of money from Fidelio Paez over the past five years. And the document was an agreement to repay the entire sum immediately.

Beads of perspiration formed on Lucy's furrowed brow. Whether this monstrous man accepted it or not, there *had* been a ghastly misunderstanding. Cindy genuinely believed that her father-in-law was rich, and if she had written asking for money it had definitely been done in the mistaken conviction that Fidelio Paez could well afford to be generous.

Fidelio was almost seventy years old. On a foreman's wages it must have taken him a lifetime to build up so healthy a savings account. Two lifetimes, Lucy adjusted, marvelling that a ranch foreman could ever have amassed such a sum. But now all that money was gone, and with it the old man's security. How on earth was such a huge amount to be repaid?

The small flat which Cindy had bought for Lucy and their late mother was already up for sale, Lucy reminded herself in a rush of relief. But even if the property fetched its full asking price it would still only cover about half of the outstanding debt. Did Cindy *own* her expensive Docklands apartment? And how much of Cindy's original inheritance at nineteen still remained intact? Any of it?

Her twin had joked that buying the flat for her sister and her mother had been a good way of preventing her from spending all her money. 'I'm too extravagant...I *know* I am, but why shouldn't I treat myself?' Cindy had asked her twin defensively. 'I just can't resist nice things. Roger gets really angry with me, but he's always had it easy. How could he understand what I went through living with Dad? Roger never had to go without food or decent clothes because his father had taken every last penny and blown it on booze!'

The memory of that revealing conversation still pierced Lucy like an accusing knife. When her twin had castigated Roger for his lack of understanding of what made her a spendthrift, she might as well have thrown in Lucy's name too. Lucy had been protected when she was a vulnerable child. Cindy had been betrayed by an adult in the grip of an addiction out of his control. And without doubt her sister still bore those scars.

'Will you sign, *señora*?' Joaquin Del Castillo challenged softly.

Lucy trembled on the brink of speech. She stifled a craven desire to tell him that he had entrapped the wrong sister. Not yet, an inner voice screeched. Impulsive speech or action would be an act of insanity with a male who had gone to such frightening lengths to corner a woman he believed to be a heartless confidence trickster. Furthermore a confession of her true identity would at this moment make him even angrier. And Lucy was no longer labouring under the naive conviction that she was dealing with some straightforward rancher from the backwoods.

The repayment agreement still tightly gripped in her hands had been drawn up by a top-flight and no doubt very expensive legal firm in the City of London. Joaquin Del Castillo had also admitted to having had enquiries made about her sister in London. All that sort of thing cost a great deal of money. Joaquin Del Castillo was also wearing what looked very much like a Rolex watch. She had noticed it the night before but had assumed that it was a cheap fake. Now she was no longer so sure. The cowboys in that ramshackle bar the day before had been doing an extraordinary amount of respectful bowing and scraping around Joaquin Del Castillo.

'Who *are* you?' Lucy questioned tautly.

'You know who I am, *señora*.'

'I know nothing about you but your name,' Lucy argued feverishly.

'It is not necessary that you should know more,' Joaquin fielded with supreme disdain. 'Now...will you sign that document?'

Lucy tilted her chin and said shakily. 'I'm not prepared to sign anything under duress.'

Shimmering green eyes raked over her pale frightened face. 'So I will call with you next week and see how you feel then,' Joaquin drawled silkily, and in one long fluid stride he turned on his heel.

'Next *week*...?' Lucy gasped incredulously, her head thumping so hard that she was beginning to feel slightly sick. 'I assume that's your idea of a joke—'

He swung back with innate grace. 'Why would I be joking?'

'You can't possibly mean that you intend to leave me here until next week!'

'Why not?'

'*Why not?* Because I don't want to be here and you've got no right to keep me here against my will...I could put the police on you for this!' Lucy sliced back frantically as she forced herself upright again on wobbling knees.

'And what crime would you then accuse me of committing, *señora*?' Joaquin Del Castillo prompted with sardonic amusement. 'You are not even on my land. You came here of your own volition and now you are taking up residence in your father-in-law's home. What do either of those actions have to do with me?'

Aghast at that subtle and devious response, and the clear forethought and planning which must have preceded it, Lucy stared at him with increasing desperation. 'I could never find my way back to San Angelita without your help!'

Joaquin shrugged without remorse. 'And you won't get it unless you sign that agreement. By the way,' he murmured in casual aside as he paused in the open doorway, 'don't waste your time trying to suborn Mateo. He speaks no English, and in common with all Fidelio's friends and well-wishers he is disgusted by what you have done!'

A cold sweat of panic breaking out on her skin, Lucy got up and hurtled dizzily through the door in his wake. 'I can't sign that agreement...I don't have that kind of money.' She stumbled clumsily over that driven admission as she gazed pleadingly up at him. 'We need to talk about this. Surely there's some other way of sorting this awful business out...'

Joaquin Del Castillo stared down at her, stunning eyes narrowed to a sliver of glinting light in his darkly handsome features. Her breath locked in her dry throat. Those spectacular eyes, scorching as the sun's heat, beat down on her. All of a sudden she felt as if a hundred trapped butterflies were going crazy inside her. Her heart crashed against her breastbone, shock shrilling through her as she trembled, paralysed to the spot by the most extraordinary rising sense of excitement.

'Some *other* way would naturally be the only way you know,' Joaquin breathed huskily, a derisive slant to his hard, compelling mouth. 'Sex is your currency and I can see that you would not find lying back under me a punishment.'

Lucy gave him an incredulous look, reeling under the onslaught of that insult.

He lowered his imperious dark head, sunlight gleaming over the glossy luxuriance of his blue-black hair. 'That air of gauche uncertainty and fragile femininity is remarkably convincing...or at least it would be if I wasn't aware that you have been the mistress of at least two wealthy married men!'

'How...*dare*...you?' Lucy gasped, cheeks aflame and incensed.

'How very easy it must have been for you to fool Mario into believing that he had found the love of his life!'

Cindy had adored Mario Paez, and had been totally gutted by his death. Sheer outrage ripped through Lucy and she flew forward, swung her arm back like a champion golfer to gain momentum, and took a violent swing at another human being for the first time ever. Joaquin sidestepped her with such speed and dexterity that she almost lost her balance and fell flat on her face. A pair of large and very powerful hands snapped around her waist and the next minute she was airborne.

Out of her head with frustrated fury as Joaquin held her at extended arm's length, with her feet dangling out of contact with solid ground, Lucy flailed her clenched fists about uselessly, because she couldn't get close enough to hit him. 'Put me down...put me down, you pig!' she screeched at him full blast.

Savagely amused green eyes raked over her hectically flushed and outraged face. 'There's also a certain piquancy to your extreme lack of size. You look like a dainty doll but you have the temper of a shrew—'

'Let go of me, you great hulking bully!' Lucy spat at him.

'*Claro!* I am seeing the *real* woman now,' Joaquin Del Castillo purred as he surveyed her, lush inky black lashes low on smouldering eyes. Raw sexuality emanated from him in unashamed waves. 'And what a tigress you must be between the sheets...all teeth and claws and hunger.'

About to launch another seething outburst at him, Lucy blinked in sheer bemusement, her soft full mouth falling open. Never before had any man addressed her in such terms. He wiped out her anger. She was more fascinated by that tantalising and false image of herself than insulted. Unwarily she clashed with those amazingly intense eyes of his and gulped. He looked like a mountain lion about to leap on a little fluffy lamb. 'No...'

'The word you use with me is *sí*...it means yes, and I like to hear it,' Joaquin Del Castillo confided in a deep dark drawl that rasped down her spine like sandpaper on silk, and he drew her in to him and banded his arms round her narrow ribcage instead. 'Say it for me...'

A strange all-pervasive ache stirred deep in Lucy's pelvis, wiping out her ability to concentrate. 'No—'

'*Sí…*' Joaquin instructed, slowly crushing her swelling breasts into the hard wall of his chest, one strong arm sliding down her back to curve round her hips and hold her fast as he studied her with flaming mesmeric intensity. '*Dios*…you will say it to please me.'

'Please you…' Lucy echoed, her entire body plastered to every vibrant masculine angle of his and assailed by a quivering seductive pliancy. Her heart was racing so fast it threatened cardiac arrest. Driven by a temptation stronger than she could resist, she raised her hand and traced the sculpted line of one slanting male cheekbone, smooth golden skin overlying a truly spectacular arrangement of bone.

His dark head lowered to capture her exploring forefinger between his lips. Lucy watched him in shaken fascination. A soft gasp was dragged from low in her convulsing throat. Every pulse in her treacherous body went crazy as he gently sucked, silken black lashes almost hitting his cheekbones. Like ice cream on a hot stove she could feel her flesh melting over her bones in a sweet, strong agony of need so new to her experience it overwhelmed her defences.

'*Sí…*' Joaquin prompted thickly as he lifted his arrogant dark head.

'*Sí…*' Lucy framed without even knowing what she was saying, utterly enthralled by the wash of agonising sensation pulsing up inside her.

He caught her parted lips with his and tasted her. Raw, burning excitement blazed up in a head-spinning tide that swept her away. Just one kiss… She had never dreamt but had often fantasised, never once expecting to experience such a response in reality. But the hard hot heat of Joaquin Del Castillo's hungry mouth on hers was a passionate revelation to Lucy. The passion he summoned up inside her controlled her utterly. She couldn't get enough of him even when the need to breathe sobbed in her deflated lungs.

'The face of a sweet Botticelli angel, the brain of a calculator and the sexual appetite of a natural whore,' Joaquin spelt out silkily, lifting his head and holding her back from him. 'It would please me to throw you down and take you here...to use you as you once used poor Mario. But I believe I can withstand the temptation.'

Lucy was shell-shocked, gasping for air. Her every nerve jangled with a sense of deprivation so strong she almost cried out in protest and grabbed him back to her again. Stunned by a complete inability to work out how she had turned into a wanton stranger in Joaquin Del Castillo's arms, and finally forced to support her own weight again, Lucy reeled dizzily. The sick pounding behind her temples made her weary mouth curl in a little moue of pain.

'Looking pathetic doesn't work with me either,' Joaquin slung down at her with grim emphasis.

Lucy focused on him hazily and noticed, really could not have helped noticing when he wore such close-fitting pants, that he was in a very masculine state of arousal. And so shaken was she by the sight of a male in that condition she stared and abstractedly recalled that he had begun the assault on her senses by doing wildly indecent things to her finger. Suddenly she was undyingly grateful that matters hadn't proceeded any further than that one breathtaking kiss, for she had no idea, absolutely no idea, just *how*... Her mother had warned her that what a woman often thought she wanted wasn't much fun once she actually got it. She was now more than ready to be convinced.

'I feel ill...' Lucy confided helplessly, swaying without even realising it and wondering why her skin still felt as if it was on fire when he was no longer touching her.

'You cannot fool me into removing you from here,' Joaquin drawled with derisive cool, his lean dark face unimpressed. 'I fully intend that you should endure the privations of what you would sentence Fidelio to endure when he is no longer fit to work.'

She wasn't well; that was what the matter was with her. In fact, she felt just as she had felt when she had had the flu a month back, only *worse*, she conceded absently. Had she imagined Joaquin Del Castillo kissing her? Why would he have kissed her? What sense did that make?

'Men don't make sense…men are animals,' Lucy announced with semi-delirious conviction, without even realising that she was talking out loud. 'You are the prime example…you are the definitive proof. I should never have argued with Mum—'

'*Madre de Dios*…' He interrupted her rambling spiel with incredulity. 'What—?'

Lucy groaned, pushing a shaking hand over her wet brow, no longer able to focus properly, just as her knees began to shake and crumple beneath her. 'Awful…feel awful—'

Joaquin Del Castillo's dusty black riding boots appeared in her vision. 'I will not be taken in by this outrageous theatrical display, *señora*.'

Lucy slumped down on one elbow. And then with a faint moan, as the world swung tipsily and blackness folded in entirely, she passed out altogether.

CHAPTER THREE

LUCY stirred and shifted. An experimental movement of her head confirmed that the awful pounding there had mercifully subsided. But even before she opened her eyes, she was assailed by a bewildering surge of powerful images.

Joaquin looking down at her, fabulous eyes green as jade, his concern palpable. Joaquin murmuring in soothing Spanish as she tossed and turned in a fever. Joaquin laughing. *Laughing?* But only for a split second. His lean dark face had swiftly shuttered again, leaving her with a sharp sense of loss. So confusing were those pictures flashing through her reawakening brain she blanked them out.

Opening her eyes, she discovered that she had not dreamt up the incredible bedroom in which she had lain since she had succumbed to her second attack of flu. Afternoon sunlight illuminated the exquisite antique furniture and the wonderful watercolours on the walls. It was a huge room. Elegant and unbelievably luxurious, right down to the solid six inches of superb lace edging the sheet beneath her hand. Her fingers stroked the lace and then stilled uncertainly again as Joaquin came back into her thoughts at the speed of a shooting star. Was this *his* house? If it was, he was a seriously wealthy male. Who was he?

Twenty-two. In spite of all her efforts to the contrary, she had got to twenty-two years of age without meeting one moment of serious temptation, Lucy conceded ruefully. And then the biggest, bossiest creep in Guatemala, who unfortunately happened to enjoy devastatingly spectacular good looks and the kind of sensual technique she had doubted even existed, had made a sexual advance on her finger. She quivered just thinking about that moment and felt her foolish tummy churn and leap at the memory of the kiss which had followed.

A bemused indent forming on her brow as she realised that she was thinking about Joaquin Del Castillo yet *again*, Lucy sat up and sent her gaze winging round the room. She needed to phone Cindy, but there was no telephone. Sliding out of bed on wobbly legs, she went into the *en suite* bathroom. Weak though she was, she headed straight for the shower cubicle.

Afterwards, she studied her reflection in the vanity mirror and heaved a sigh over her pale face and the childishly curly torrent of caramel-blonde ringlets forming as her hair dried. She smoothed a hand over the mint-green nightdress she wore. It was beautiful, and, like everything else she had brought to Guatemala, it belonged to her sister. Light as silk and whisper-thin, the fabric moulded every female curve and was a far cry from the cotton jersey nightwear which Lucy usually favoured.

Freshening up had tired her out again. She walked slowly over to the bedroom windows. There she froze in her tracks, for the view beyond those windows made her head swim afresh. She clutched at the tassel-edged curtain to steady herself, shut her eyes and opened them again, but still that breathtaking vision of steep, lush forested green slopes and wildly colourful tropical vegetation confronted her stunned gaze. She could hear but only now recognise the cries of exotic birds which had become eerily familiar during her illness. Surely such a fantastic and exotic landscape could not exist close to Fidelio Paez's little stucco retirement home? Where on earth was she?

'Welcome to the most *boring* place on earth...' A female voice murmured drily from behind her.

Startled, Lucy spun round so fast she staggered slightly. A tall stunning brunette with smooth black hair and a perfect oval face was studying her from the far side of the room. Her short strappy silver dress and her jewelled choker exuded designer chic and sophistication.

'Hacienda de Oro…literally the House of Gold. The conservationist's paradise, the archaeologist's dream destination…but the It Girl's living death,' the self-possessed brunette completed, with a dissatisfied twist of her sultry mouth.

'The It Girl's living death…?' Lucy repeated weakly, not quite sure she had heard her correctly.

'I'm Yolanda Del Castillo, Joaquin's sister. Surely you know what an It Girl is?'

Lucy nodded, but only slowly. She had read about the cult of the new It Girls in newspapers. Young, rich, high society British women, who were wildly popular with the media. They partied from dawn to dusk, wore fabulous clothes and dated only the most newsworthy men. Such an existence was so far removed from Lucy's own that she just stared at Yolanda Del Castillo, who undeniably seemed to possess all the attributes it took to be an It Girl, continually photographed, pursued and envied. Even in daylight, it seemed, Yolanda dressed as if she was about to go to a party.

'You speak wonderful English,' Lucy remarked, awkward in the presence of such exoticism.

Yolanda uttered a rueful groan. 'Where do you think I was educated?'

Most probably in a British school, Lucy gathered, feeling foolish.

'Where is this house?' Lucy pressed.

'You're still in the Petén, just a different part of it.'

'So how did I get here?' Lucy asked.

'Joaquin had you airlifted in.'

'Airlifted?' Lucy interrupted helplessly. 'Who are you people?'

'You really *don't* know, do you?' Yolanda rolled her
dark eyes in dramatic disbelief, momentarily looking much
younger than the twenty-two or twenty-three which Lucy
had estimated her to be. She threw the bedroom door wide
again. 'Hang on a minute—'

'Yolanda…is there a phone I could use?' Lucy hastened
to ask, before Joaquin's sister could disappear again.

Yolanda's attention shifted to the vacant spot by the bed.
She frowned in surprise. 'Well, I don't see *why* you
shouldn't have a phone!' she remarked with instant sympathy. 'You may be a con-artist, but for Joaquin to have
the phone removed is total sensory deprivation! I couldn't
exist for five minutes without a phone!'

Lucy turned white as milk. 'You *know*…I mean—?'

'You thought I didn't just 'cos I came in to chat?'
Yolanda shrugged a languid shoulder. 'I'm bored out of my
mind here without company. But I know what you did…
Of course I know, and it was disgusting! Fidelio is the
sweetest old man.'

Cut to the bone by that blunt condemnation from yet
another source, and feeling as limp as a wrung-out dishrag,
Lucy sank down on the edge of the bed. Within minutes
Yolanda reappeared, to toss a glossy magazine down beside
her.

'Fidelio Paez started working for my family when he was
fifteen, *señora*,' Yolanda informed her with cool dignity.
'We threw a big retirement party for him. Imagine how we
felt when we later found out that Fidelio had gone to work
for a neighbour because he was too embarrassed to ask
Joaquin if he could continue working for us!'

'And then Fidelio told your brother what had happened
to his savings,' Lucy assumed uncomfortably.

'No! Fidelio has no idea that you cheated him out of his
money,' Yolanda contradicted instantly. 'Joaquin had to do
his own detective work.'

In considerable discomfiture, Lucy dropped her head.

'And while we're on the subject of my brother, stop embarrassing me by making a total ass of yourself around him!'

Her lips parting company in sheer shock, Lucy looked up.

'The way you were carrying on when you were ill, I initially thought that Joaquin had brought his mistress home!' Yolanda admitted in exasperation.

'His...m-mistress?' Lucy stammered with incredulity.

'All Joaquin's mistresses have been foreigners like you. Guatemalan women don't sleep around. We know better,' the brunette told her with unapologetic superiority.

'What way was I...''carrying on''?' Lucy tilted her chin, denying the charge.

'OK, so you had a fever, but you were continually moaning on about how beautiful Joaquin's eyes were and asking him to kiss you...talk about deeply uncool! Listening outside that door, I was just *cringing* for you!'

A tide of truly painful colour illuminating her face, Lucy turned her shaken gaze away from her visitor in self-protection. Suddenly her eyes were stinging with stupid tears.

Yolanda walked round the bed to get a better look at her victim and frowned in frank bewilderment. 'You know, you just don't add up...you are acting *so* wet!'

Lucy chewed at her wobbly lower lip. 'I'm only feeling weepy because I've been ill—'

'No...you fancy my brother something rotten,' the brunette countered, unimpressed, and she shook her head in wondering pity. 'I have problems, but you have got an even *bigger* problem, Lucy!'

The door snapped shut on Yolanda's departure. Drawing in a deep shuddering breath, Lucy lifted the magazine she had left behind. Her hands were trembling and she felt as

weak as a kitten. But, worst of all, she felt utterly humiliated. A con-artist who had made an ass of herself?
Evidently while her temperature had been high she had
rambled on like some dizzy teenager suffering from a severe crush.

The cover of the magazine bore a picture of Joaquin
emerging from a limousine with a very beautiful blonde.
Lucy leafed through and found the relevant page. It was a
North American magazine dedicated to depicting the lives
of the rich and famous. Correction, Lucy adjusted as she
slowly scanned the pages of photos, the lives of the *super-
rich*...

For Joaquin Del Castillo appeared to own a whole se-
lection of homes around the globe. There were several shots
of various enormous properties, sheltering behind high
walls and huge gates. Her heart beating very fast, Lucy
skimmed through the brief blurb for actual facts. Joaquin
was variously described as a 'billionaire industrialist' and
a 'reformed playboy', who now spent much of his time
advising governments on conservation. He was thirty years
old, single, and he changed women like he changed his
shirts. His late father hadn't married for the first time until
he was sixty, and there was strong speculation that Joaquin
was planning to do the same.

Lucy snapped shut the magazine again. So, a gorgeous
billionaire had kissed her! Where had that naff thought
come from? Mortified by her rebellious mind, which refused to focus on what was truly important, Lucy instead
pondered the likely power at Joaquin's fingertips. Her blood
duly chilled. Cindy had made a very dangerous enemy who
had the resources to cause a great deal of trouble.

Since she was now totally exhausted, and in no state to
leave her room in search of a phone, Lucy crawled back
into bed, sinking beneath the cool sheets to close her eyes
in weary relief.

*   *   *

'Lucy…?'

Even as Lucy surfaced from sleep again every fibre in her body knew that the speaker was Joaquin, for nobody else had ever managed to make her name sound that exciting. That wonderful sexy drawl, rich as honey with smoky overtones, haunted her dreams, so she kept her eyes shut, warding off temptation as best she could.

'Go 'way,' she mumbled in sleepy self-defence.

'Wake up, Lucy…'

With drowsy reluctance, Lucy focused on the male poised at the foot of her bed. It was dusk. But, even in that duller light, his dark-as-midnight hair gleamed with vitality and his fabulous eyes glittered like jewels. That Joaquin should always look spectacular was no longer any surprise to Lucy, for other memories were stirring to endow him with a familiarity she accepted without question. Joaquin had been with her when the fever had been at its worst. Whenever she had become momentarily conscious of her surroundings again Joaquin had been there.

With a sigh, Lucy stretched to loosen her muscles. Belatedly conscious of the tension zapping through the air, she glanced up and connected with the direction of Joaquin's intent gaze. As she dropped her own attention to the straining mounds of her breasts, now so clearly delineated beneath her nightdress, she froze in dismay. Mortified by the provocative display she had unintentionally made of herself, Lucy flushed a rosy red and grabbed at the sheet to tug it up over her scantily clad frame.

Joaquin tilted back his proud dark head and continued to look at her levelly. However, his handsome mouth had now taken on a distinctly cynical twist. 'You're obviously feeling much better.'

'Would you mind telling me exactly where I am?' Lucy was breathless and hugely self-conscious, and desperate just to fill the silence.

'In one of my guestrooms,' Joaquin imparted with formidable cool. 'It is three days since you fell ill.'

'You're wearing a suit...' Lucy noted inconsequentially, taking in the beautifully tailored cream linen sheathing his lithe powerful physique. The shade merely enhanced his dark and vibrant animal magnetism. Her brain refused to dwell on one thought for longer than two seconds. She watched his sleek and aggressive jawline clench. 'And you seem so...so constrained...' She noted this to herself in instinctive confusion, for she could not help but contrast his concern when she had been ill to his current frozen demeanour.

Volatile green eyes flashed down at her in flaring anger. 'Let me tell you what I am repressing, *señora*,' Joaquin Del Castillo spelt out, the deep-freeze act fracturing fast. 'A near overpowering desire to drag your scrawny little body out of that comfortable bed and make you dig ditches and sweat in honest labour as you deserve!'

Sprung finally from all introspection, Lucy flinched and paled.

'Indeed it is a great challenge for me to treat you with the consideration due to an invalid,' Joaquin Del Castillo admitted in a driven undertone. 'But I wish to impress on you that I never at any stage intended you to suffer harm or injury. The doctor believes that you were not very fit to begin with. Had I been aware that you were genuinely as physically frail and weak as you appeared, I would have ensured that the journey you underwent to Fidelio's home was less taxing.'

He could use an awful lot of words without actually grasping the nettle and apologising, Lucy registered. For of course, she conceded with the sense of hindsight, that long arduous ride must have been completely unnecessary to a male with Joaquin Del Castillo's financial resources. Even

she knew that a four-wheel drive could have traversed so
flat a terrain with ease.

'Is it your wish that I contact your fiancé to inform him
that you have been ill?' Joaquin enquired icily.

A blank look flowered in Lucy's eyes. 'But I don't have
a fiancé...'

Joaquin stiffened, and then surveyed her with sudden intense derision. 'So you have jilted Roger Harkness! I noticed that you wore no ring and I should have guessed. He
was the one aspect of your lifestyle which failed to make
sense. Why would a woman with your expensive tastes
choose to marry a newly qualified accountant?'

Recalling too late that she was supposed to be pretending
to *be* Cindy, and deeply shaken that he should be aware
not only that her sister was engaged but also of the identity
and occupation of her fiancé, Lucy gasped. 'I...I—'

'*Dios*...so you were only playing with Harkness?
Amusing yourself while you waited for your next rich pro-
tector to come along?' Joaquin Del Castillo assumed with
contemptuous distaste. 'You have deprived me of the pleasure of telling him exactly what you are, for no man should
take such a bride without forewarning!'

An anxious burst of low-pitched Spanish interrupted him.
A stout little woman with grey hair had come into the room.
She wasted no time in sliding a thermometer between
Lucy's lips. Studying the younger woman's drawn face and
anxious eyes, she glanced at her employer in speaking re-
proach.

Lucy watched Joaquin's powerful chest swell with the
effort it took to bite back his temper. His expressive mouth
compressed into a bloodless line of rock-steady restraint,
but slight colour now delineated the hard jut of his high
cheekbones. With an inclination of his imperious dark head,
he squared his broad shoulders. 'We will discuss this matter
again when you are stronger,' he informed her glacially.

Like a fish let off the hook at the very last moment, Lucy felt her tension evaporate, and she slumped back against the comfortable pillows. An hour later, as she dined from a tray set with exquisite porcelain, fine crystal and solid silver salt and pepper shakers, she perfectly understood Joaquin Del Castillo's outrage at the situation in which he now found himself.

He had brought her to Guatemala to confront and punish her. He had intended to corner her into signing that repayment agreement by marooning her in Fidelio's isolated home and making her rough it. Yet here she was, lying back against freshly laundered pillows being waited on hand and foot. Only the very rich could afford such a level of service. And the more Lucy pictured Joaquin's lean dark aristocratic face, the more she marvelled that she had not instantly recognised that blazing aura of power and expectation for what it was.

She really had to get hold of a phone and warn Cindy. That had now become a matter of even greater urgency. 'No man should take such a bride without forewarning'. The memory of that devastating assurance from Joaquin filled Lucy with fear on her sister's behalf. Cindy's wedding was only a few weeks away. Very probably Joaquin knew that date as well. His continuing belief that *she* was Cindy, but no longer a bride-to-be, was currently her sister's only protection from such a vengeful act.

With decision, Lucy got out of bed. It was after ten in the evening. Hopefully most of the occupants of the house would be downstairs. The wrap that matched her nightdress lay across a chair. Donning it, she crept out of her room into a long well-lit corridor with a highly polished wooden floor adorned at intervals with superb woven rugs. She passed by closed doors with her nerves humming a tattoo that made the hair on her nape prickle with forboding.

It was an enormous house. From the mouth of the corridor she peered out on to an impressive gallery with a ceiling that soared high above, hearing first the distant echo of voices and then quick steps traversing the hall which she assumed lay below. Several feet from her, she noticed a door lying ajar. On tiptoe, she approached, listened, and, hearing nothing, gently pushed the door wider.

Seeing that the bedroom, which was even more grand than her own, was empty, she hurriedly checked that there *was* a telephone before quietly closing the door behind her again to ensure that she would not be overheard. Since sneaking about like a cat burglar did not come naturally to Lucy, her heart was now beating so fast that it was threatening to choke her. She switched on the massive lamp behind the phone.

At speed she punched out the number of her sister's apartment, praying that her twin was at home. The instant Cindy heard her voice, she laughed, and said brightly, 'I suppose you've been having too good a time to call before this!'

'Don't I *wish*!' Lucy groaned, and sucked in a deep calming breath before she continued, 'I've landed into a really serious situation here, Cindy.'

In as few words as possible, she then hurried to tell her twin what she had to be told about her father-in-law Fidelio Paez's predicament.

However, it was a very difficult dialogue. Cindy kept on interrupting, first with ringing cries of disbelief and argument and finally with growing anger and resentment.

'Mario showed me a photo of the most incredible big ranch house...and he was staying in a five-star hotel suite when we met. Was he lying to me...*deliberately* lying about his background? Explain that to me!'

'Look, I know nothing about that end of it,' Lucy admitted unhappily, and as once again she repeated the cold facts which Joaquin had laid before her, a thunderous silence began to build at the other end of the line in London.

'If Fidelio couldn't afford to give me all that cash, he shouldn't have sent it,' Cindy finally framed in a cool, brittle voice which sounded alien to her anxiously waiting twin.

'Cindy…Joaquin Del Castillo wants that money repaid. At least there'll be the proceeds of the flat you bought for Mum and me…hopefully it will sell soon,' Lucy pointed out awkwardly in the seething quiet. 'Is there anything more left of that insurance pay-out you got when you were nineteen?'

'Do you seriously expect me to leave myself as poor as a church mouse over this nonsense?' Cindy demanded shrilly.

'As much as possible of Fidelio's money has to be returned to him—'

'I didn't *steal* that rotten money, nor did I *borrow* it! I asked and Fidelio gave, and I'm very sorry if he's broke now, but that's not my fault and it's not my responsibility either!' Cindy practically shouted, her increasing panic at what she was being told audible.

'Cindy—'

'This guy Del Castillo has really got to you, hasn't he? Well, you can stop talking about handing over what the sale of the flat brings in because Roger's expecting to put that money towards a house, and I can't tell him about all this nonsense…I *can't*!'

'It's not nonsense, Cindy. Joaquin Del Castillo is a very rich and powerful man and I don't think he'll let this matter drop—'

'If he's so darned rich, let *him* repay the money! No wonder rich people are rich,' Cindy cried wildly. 'They hang onto what they've got!'

There was a jarring noise, as if the phone handset at the

other end had been thrown down, but the line had not been disconnected. In the background, Lucy could hear her unfortunate twin giving way to angry sobs. Lucy hung on to her receiver, hoping that her sister would return to the call she had abandoned and start speaking to her again. Maybe crying would help Cindy to calm down, Lucy told herself, but there was no denying that her twin's outraged and defiant response had been an unpleasant surprise.

But possibly she had been hugely naive to expect any other reaction, Lucy reflected guiltily, belatedly struggling to put herself in her twin's place. Cindy had just received an awful shock. The news of Fidelio Paez's true station in life had shattered her sister. Cindy had sincerely believed that her father-in-law was a wealthy man. And if Cindy now had to replace Fidelio's savings, she would be surrendering the financial security she had learnt to take for granted in recent years. Nor had her sister any hope of concealing her changed circumstances from the man she was soon to marry.

Roger, stolid and conservative, Roger, who was prone to giving her sister lectures on money management. Roger, whom Cindy had already admitted was in the dark as to certain aspects of her past. Oh, dear heaven, what a dreadful, dreadful mess, Lucy conceded, her heart twisting over the situation her twin was now in. No wonder Cindy was panicking! How was Roger likely to handle this ghastly business breaking just before their wedding took place?

As Lucy hovered, literally frozen to the spot as she grasped what must now be her twin's deepest fear, it was a great relief when her sister returned to the phone again.

'Lucy…?' Cindy wailed chokily. 'What am I going to do?'

Lucy murmured as soothingly as she could, 'We'll work this out somehow. I'll get a job and help—'

'*After* the wedding!' Cindy broke in to stress tremu-

lously. 'Promise me that you'll keep this Del Castillo guy
in the dark and occupied until my wedding is safely over.'

Lucy paled at that demand. 'But...but, Cindy—'

'Roger will dump me if I tell him about this now...any
man would! I've gone from being a good catch to a liabil-
ity, and if I was Roger I know I'd run, because I'm going
to be living off him now and I'm no good at budgeting!'
Cindy sobbed out, becoming more hysterical with every
passing second. 'Promise me, Lucy...*promise me*!'

An instant later, although she could see many potential
pitfalls in continuing such a deceptive course of action,
Lucy heard herself uttering reluctant agreement. How could
she urge Cindy to tell her future husband the truth in advance of their wedding? Suppose Roger *did* break off their
engagement? Lucy didn't want to carry the blame for that
development.

'Whatever happens, don't call me again,' Cindy urged in
a frantically nervous surge. 'Oh, yes, and whatever you do,
don't sign that repayment agreement in my name!'

'Sign in your name...?' Lucy repeated in a strangled
tone, because she would never have dreamt of forging her
twin's signature on any document.

'I must say he has a nerve, expecting me to come up
with the whole sum. The best I can offer is a ten-year
instalment plan!' Cindy asserted bitterly.

'I'll try to sort something out—'

'But don't you run the smallest risk of Del Castillo finding out that there are *two* of us,' Cindy warned fearfully.
'And if you can't make it back in time for the wedding,
don't worry about it...as long as my bridegroom turns up,
I'll be OK!'

A split second later, the connection was cut.

Having replaced the phone, Lucy was just drawing in
slow, sustaining oxygen when the bedroom door opened.
She almost died of fright on the spot. Dropping down on

her knees, she grabbed at the fancy fringed valance which
swept down to the carpet, intending to conceal herself under the bed. Unfortunately, the mahogany bedframe she exposed went to within a couple of inches of the floor.

As she heard Joaquin's awesomely familiar drawl re-
spond to whoever he was speaking to, either in the corridor
or just inside the bedroom—for she couldn't see where he
was now that she had dropped down below the level of the
bed—absolute panic took hold of her. Feverishly scanning
the nearest furniture for a potential hiding place and seeing
nowhere, she listened, horrorstruck, to his conversation
coming to an end. The door thudded shut. Lucy flattened
herself to the carpet and stopped breathing altogether.

A phone buzzed; not the phone by the bed. Possibly a
portable. Joaquin answered it. He didn't speak long and
concluded the call in a rather impatient tone. It finally
dawned on Lucy that she was in Joaquin's bedroom. But it
was early yet, she reasoned, maybe he would just go back
downstairs again. Surely he didn't go to bed before eleven
in the evening? Going by the pictorial evidence of his social
life in that magazine, Joaquin Del Castillo was the It Girl's
male equivalent, ungiven to the sobriety of early nights.

She listened to the soft slither of cloth against cloth and
then just cringed. He was getting undressed. But as long as
there remained the smallest chance of her creeping out
again unseen, Lucy preferred to stay where she was. How
could she possibly emerge from hiding now and make any
credible excuse for her behaviour? Another door opened.
Another light went on. Her hope of escaping undetected
rose high. He was in the *en suite* bathroom! Just as Lucy
was about to crawl to the corner of the bed and make a
break for freedom, a pair of bare brown male feet appeared
in the path of her vision.

'Are you planning to join me in the shower?' Joaquin
drawled the enquiry, his intonation smooth as black velvet.

CHAPTER FOUR

IN SHATTERED receipt of that slumbrous invitation, and the obvious fact that Joaquin Del Castillo had been aware all along that she was cowering on the floor on the far side of his bed, Lucy's tongue just glued fast to the roof of her dry mouth. 'I...I...'

Slowly, she lifted her head, so engulfed by embarrassment that she didn't know where to put herself, wildly wishing herself anywhere but the place she now was. At his feet in her nightie in *his* bedroom late at night! His fine white linen shirt hung unbuttoned and loose over his well-cut beige trousers, revealing a powerful torso, and his pectoral muscles were lightly defined by rough dark curls of hair. His skin was the colour of rich honey. Presented with that impressive expanse of male chest, she tried and failed to swallow.

'Even from the door, I can see over the bed, *querida*. I'm a lot taller than you are,' Joaquin said drily.

Maybe that crack about sharing his shower was some sort of Central American joke, Lucy decided, it not occurring to her for one moment that he could possibly have been serious. As he reached down a lean brown hand to close it over hers and pull her upright, she looked up and collided with those extraordinary black-fringed green eyes head-on. Whoosh...it was like falling on an electric current! Whatever desperate excuse might have been struggling for utterance on her tongue evaporated from her brain like Scotch mist.

'Lucy...Lucy,' Joaquin chided silkily in that dark, deep

sensual accent of his, curving long brown fingers over her
sensitive jawbone.

Her head felt light. The butterflies in her tummy were
back. She could feel every tiny muscle she possessed
tauten, even her skin tightening over her bones. But this
time she recognised what was happening to her. She saw
into the dark secret heart of that surge of excitement rising
and her breath snarled up in her throat in shock.

'Don't tell me you've lost your nerve,' Joaquin prompted
lazily, his intent gaze scanning her upturned face.

In turn, Lucy was helplessly studying him. The high
cheekbones which gave his lean features such proud defi-
nition, the cool, straight dark brows, the strong nose, hard
jawline and wonderfully shaped mouth. 'You fancy my
brother something rotten,' Yolanda had said, and Lucy finally acknowledged just how right his sister had been. A
wash of colour burned her cheeks, for she felt the full
weight of her own foolishness.

'No, I—'

Joaquin elevated a satiric dark brow. 'You weren't expecting me this soon, *es verdad*?'

Desperately trying to wrench herself free of the effect he
was having on her, Lucy made a huge effort to concentrate.
But she couldn't work out what he was talking about, which
scarcely helped. 'I don't—'

'*No importa…*' His brilliant green gaze shimmered.

As she collided afresh with that searching scrutiny, her
heart started to race. Sense told her to move, but the whirring tension in the air was the most deliciously seductive
sensation. Paralysed to the spot in mesmerised stillness, she
could feel her pulses racing, the very blood coursing
through her veins. He was so close to her she could smell
the hot vibrant scent of him, and it made her head spin and
her body quiver with the kind of longing that left her weak.

The silence thickened to an almost unbearable level.

His bright gaze narrowed. Lifting his hand, he tugged loose the ribbon tie of the wrap she wore. It was done in such an entirely natural way that she simply stood there as he tipped the silky wrap from her shoulders and let it slide down into a pool at her feet. 'Joaquin…what on earth?' she whispered, just a split second too late.

In answer, Joaquin gave her a wolfish smile. Settling his hands on her taut shoulders, he lowered his proud dark head. She knew he was going to kiss her. Sheer anticipation wiped her mind clear of all else. She just wanted him to *do* it! In fact she could hardly wait: it was like a tremendously important test. The last time he had kissed her, she had had a fever. And ever since then she had wondered and wondered whether she had truly felt what she remembered.

With a smoky laugh that acknowledged the height differential between them, Joaquin sank down on the side of the bed and tugged her towards him. Then he slid his hands to her hips and lifted her on to his lap. What are you *doing*? a little voice screamed in the back of her bemused brain.

'No, this isn't… Well, it isn't…' Lucy began tremulously as self-consciousness and a sense of events moving too rapidly out of her control almost freed her of the spell he cast.

Unconcerned by such minor mutterings, Joaquin settled her down on him. He spread long graceful fingers to cup her cheekbones and she was lost again. Meeting those beautiful crystal-clear eyes of his, she just wanted to fling herself at him. Her whole quivering body was poised on a wild high. Her breasts were full, their straining peaks almost painfully sensitive. At the heart of her there was the most intense ache.

'You understand…*this* has nothing to do with Fidelio,' Joaquin warned her in a roughened undertone.

'Kiss me…' Lucy urged, all shyness put to flight by the agony of eagerness clawing up inside her.

And he did. Slowly and thoroughly and with the sort of smooth sensual expertise that she was defenceless against. Yet she sought no defence. He pried apart her lips and used the tip of his tongue in a teasing darting foray into the tender interior of her mouth. She almost passed out from the fierce surge of excitement he generated. Her hands broke the hold of his so that she could wrap her arms round him.

'Witch…' Joaquin husked with sensual fervour, before he took that invitation and possessed her mouth again with wild hot hunger.

Like oil thrown on embers, that hunger set Lucy alight. As he drew her down on to the bed she let her fingers sink into the thick dark strands of his hair. With a growling sound deep in his throat, he rolled over and came down on her. The heat and weight of his long powerful body on hers added a whole new dimension to the experience. With every seeking intimate thrust of his tongue which imitated a far more intimate possession Lucy burned. She was so hooked on that raw, drugging charge of ever-rising excitement she could barely breathe. His hands stroked her breasts, expert fingers teasing at a tender tip, making her moan her response under the onslaught on his mouth, all control abandoned.

A knock sounded on the bedroom door. Lucy didn't hear it, but Joaquin wrenched himself free of her with shocking abruptness. She felt that, and could hardly have remained unaware of the change in mood when she found herself being unceremoniously dumped back on to the carpet and told to stay there.

She was even more startled then to hear Yolanda, speaking in her own language several feet away. Only then did she lower her spinning head in shaken dismay at her own behaviour. Even as the unmistakable sound of an argument between brother and sister took place at the door, with the brunette's voice growing ever more shrill and angry while Joaquin's grew ever colder and steadier, Lucy just sat where she was, staring into space with shocked eyes.

She was still trembling, and deeply conscious of the after-pains of such unbridled passion. That hot greedy craving was still inside her, taking no account of place or person or indeed anything but its own existence. Her body wanted Joaquin Del Castillo. *She* wanted Joaquin, she adjusted in raw mortification. Until that moment she had never understood just how frighteningly powerful such physical need could be. And how could she blame him for taking advantage of her scantily clad presence in his bedroom? She had just let him...indeed had actively encouraged him to make love to her.

The noisy tap-tap of high heels stalking away penetrated Lucy's reverie.

'One down, one to go,' Joaquin spelt out, bending down to scoop her off the carpet with grim determination.

'One down...one *what*?' Lucy gasped.

'You're going back to your own bed!' His high proud cheekbones scored with dark colour, and his eyes bright and hard as emeralds, Joaquin raked her pink face with angry derision.

'Of course I am,' Lucy mumbled, every vowel sound strangulated by an inability to come up with any other response. Even she was prepared to concede that but for his sister's interruption where she herself was to spend the night might reasonably have been in doubt.

'*Of course?*' Joaquin stressed with stinging scorn as he strode to the door. 'I can't believe that I almost fell for that cheap seduction routine!'

'I...I b-beg your pardon?' Lucy stammered.

'*Por Dios*…you know what you are about with a man…you brought me close enough to the edge!'

'Don't you dare talk to me like that!'

Having made the return trip to her bedroom in record time, Joaquin dumped her back down on her comfortable bed. She fell back against the tumbled pillows, her caramel-blonde hair spilling round her hectically flushed heart-shaped face, her violet eyes bright with chagrin.

'There *was* no seduction routine!' Lucy spluttered.

'You were waiting for me.' With brooding intensity, Joaquin stared down at her, eyes a glimmering crystalline flash below lush black lashes. 'With my kid sister under the same roof…have you no decency?'

In receipt of that continuing appraisal, Lucy was startled to feel her entire skin surface burn with a sensation that was far from being the shame it should have been. Excitement still shimmered in the air between them like a barrier begging to be broken. It was impossible for her to defend herself against his accusation without revealing that she had been using his phone. If she admitted that, he might check out the number and discover that she had called what should have been her own empty London apartment.

'Obviously not,' she heard herself confirm, thrilling in the strangest way to that image of herself as a sexually confident and immorally manipulative female.

Goaded by that response, Joaquin came down on the side of the bed and leant over her. 'So you admit that?'

His brilliant eyes clashed with hers. Invisible sparks seemed to fly up. Her breath caught in her throat. 'I admit nothing,' she muttered unevenly, every sense quickening to his proximity.

Joaquin reached out a hand and slowly wound his fingers into a whole handful of her glossy ringlets. His astonishing eyes never left hers for a second. 'I swear you will not profit by my desire for you, *querida*,' he asserted in a dangerous growl.

But even the danger excited Lucy. To be desired was to feel like a seductive stranger inside her own homely skin. Her tongue snaked out to moisten her dry lips. She watched his attention drop to the moist fullness of her pink mouth and she trembled. A pin would have sounded like a rock falling in the charged silence which now stretched between them.

'Oh, dear…I didn't realise you still needed to be tucked in at night, Lucy,' Yolanda remarked in dulcet surprise from the doorway.

Joaquin drew back from Lucy and slowly sprang upright. His beautiful mouth quirking with what could have been suppressed amusement, he veiled his gaze and walked out of the room with a cool aside in soft Spanish to his sibling.

'*Buenas noches*, Lucy,' his sister sighed, looking nothing at all like the kid he had styled her as, she cast a martial glance of reproof in Lucy's direction.

Embarrassed to have been surprised that close to Joaquin, and enveloped in a burning blush, Lucy scrambled under the sheets with a muttered goodnight of her own. But she lay back unable to sleep. In twenty-two years she had never felt so *alive* as she had felt in Joaquin Del Castillo's arms. That was a pretty pathetic admission, she decided, reluctantly forced to admit to her own slender experience of men.

At school she had always been too quiet to interest any of the boys she'd liked. She had been nineteen when she met Steve. She had fallen head over heels for him when he came to work at the library. They had often lunched together and he had seemed to really enjoy being with her. But she had totally misunderstood the precise tenor of his interest and she had been devastated when it had finally dawned on her that Steve was gay. He had thought of her as a friend, no more, and had assumed that she knew that his flatmate was rather *more* than a friend.

The following year she had met Larry, an engineering student, who had been keen enough to ignore her excuses about not being able to go out in the evening and who had eventually just turned up on the doorstep. Sadly, his interest in Lucy had not been strong enough to prevent him from taking furious offence at her mother's extremely rude and contemptuous reception. And that had been the end of that.

Little wonder that in Joaquin Del Castillo's radius Lucy was now becoming painfully conscious of her own naivety. For too long she had been denied the independence to make her own choices in life. Naturally that lack of experience had left its mark. As her mother's carer she had had to be mature beyond her years, but in so many other fields, she was now discovering, she was still as unsure of herself as an adolescent.

So it was hardly surprising, she reasoned feverishly, that she didn't recognise the wanton female she turned into around Joaquin. When had she ever had the chance to express that side of her nature? She was a normal flesh and blood woman and it was natural that she should want to…should want to flatten him to the bed and *rip* his clothes off? She cringed, but that was how she had felt.

But was it also natural that when Joaquin entered the same room her brain went into freefall? Natural that she should totally forget that she was supposed to be pretending to be her sister every time he looked at her or touched her? Was sexual attraction that intense and all-consuming? Or was it just that she had been living like a nun for too long so that she was now, as Yolanda had so succinctly put it, making a total ass of herself around Joaquin Del Castillo?

Where were her wits? Lucy asked herself fiercely. What had she so far done to try and sort out this gruesome situation concerning Fidelio's money? One big fat nothing, she conceded, shame and guilt engulfing her. This very day she had seen Joaquin on two separate occasions and she hadn't even raised the subject, never mind tried to talk him round into agreeing to a workable solution. Tomorrow, she promised herself, she would do what she *should* have been doing from the start...

As soon as Lucy had had breakfast the following morning, she got dressed. The contents of the suitcase that had been left behind at the bar at San Angelita now hung in the wardrobe, freshly pressed and pristine.

Lucy chose a pale blue suit. The skirt was short, the jacket very fitted, but it was a smart combination and infinitely better than wafting around in skimpy nightwear, she told herself censoriously. No wonder Joaquin had picked up the wrong signals from her! She could scarcely condemn him for assuming that she was the sort of woman who was willing to employ sex as a persuader. Now that she was properly garbed, he would naturally take her far more seriously.

Her strappy shoes were so perilously high that it was a challenge to descend the stairs with grace. Yolanda was crossing the magnificent big hall below, looking stunning but also a little startling in an incredibly tight scarlet skirt and a beaded crop top adorned with strategic cut-outs.

'Good morning,' Lucy said awkwardly to attract the brunette's attention. 'Could you tell me where I could find your brother?'

Yolanda whirled round with a frown. 'In his office, down there...' She stabbed the air with an imperious hand to indicate the branch corridor at the rear of the hall. 'But I don't think it would be a good idea to bother him right now!'

'Why?'

The volatile brunette focused smouldering dark eyes on

her and ignored the question to ask another. 'Do you have a father, Lucy?'

'He's dead—'

'A brother?'

Lucy shook her head in denial.

Yolanda's sultry mouth compressed. 'Then how could you *ever* understand our macho-dominated culture?' she demanded with unconcealed bitterness. 'A Guatemalan woman must obey first her father, then her brother, and finally her husband. All male relatives take precedence over her. What I want doesn't come into it. No, I must *still* do as I am told, like a little child! Have you any idea how that feels?'

Involuntarily, Lucy heard the echo of her late mother's constant controlling criticisms which had marked out very effective boundaries in every area of her own life.

'Lucy, you're not a teenager any more and you look ridiculous in that dress...'

'Lucy, only street-walkers wear make-up like that...'

'Lucy, you're not bright enough to go to university...'

'Lucy, how can you expect me to sit here on my own while you go to some silly evening class...how can you be so selfish?'

'I know *exactly* how it feels,' Lucy heard herself whisper.

In the act of already moving away, Yolanda turned back in surprise at that confirmation.

'My mother was rather...er...domineering,' Lucy confided in a rush.

Their eyes met in a moment of shared understanding. This time Lucy turned away first, feeling horribly disloyal for having expressed that opinion.

'My mother remarried soon after my father died and had a new family,' Yolanda framed curtly. 'I was in the way, so I was sent off to school.'

Lucy stilled, and would have responded, but Yolanda grimaced. 'Poor little me!' she completed with cool self-mockery, and started up the grand staircase.

As Lucy headed in the direction which Yolanda had indicated, she recalled that brother and sister had been arguing the previous night as well. At least, the brunette had been arguing, she adjusted, for Joaquin had stayed cool as ice. But Lucy's sympathy quite naturally lay with Yolanda. Since she herself found standing up to powerful personalities an enormous challenge, she assumed Joaquin's sister had a similar problem, worsened by a cultural bias which suggested that women were not the equal of their male counterparts. And there was no denying that Joaquin Del Castillo laid down the law like a born autocrat.

She knocked on the door and then, after waiting a moment, opened it. The room was large and imposing, more of a library than an office, with the bookshelves and the darker decor imposing a pervasively male ambience.

Joaquin had already risen from behind an immaculately tidy desk. Across the room, French doors stood wide on the lush grounds. Sunshine flooded in, gleaming over his black hair, luxuriant as polished silk. Even in the more casual garb of a short-sleeved white shirt and cream chinos, Joaquin contrived to look incredibly exclusive. The beautiful cut of his clothing exuded faultless designer tailoring and elegance. His deep-set bright eyes arrowed in on her and narrowed, his lean, dark forceful face settling into impassivity.

Lucy's heart sank in the forbidding silence which he allowed to continue. Her nervous tension increased. She dragged in a foreshortened breath. 'We need to talk about Fidelio's money,' she pointed out tautly, hating the note of apology she could hear in her own uncertain voice.

'I have already said all that I have to say on that subject,' Joaquin countered with intimidating authority and finality.

'When you sign that document, you may go home. You have no other options.'

'But there's *got* to be another option…it would be impossible to come up with that much money all at once!' Lucy protested in a burst of desperation.

Joaquin looked hugely unimpressed by that plea of poverty.

Lucy bit at her lower lip. 'Surely the offer of a substantial first payment followed by instalments would be sufficient proof of good intentions?'

'Without a legal agreement, you would back out on the promise as soon as you got back to London,' Joaquin responded very drily.

'No, I wouldn't. There's actually a property of…er… mine up for sale at the moment—'

'The only property you own is the one you live in, and it's not on the market.'

So he *didn't* know about the flat which Cindy had bought for her mother and her sister. No, of course he didn't know! Had that connection been made, he might well have discovered that Cindy had an identical twin. So persisting on the subject of that property could be downright dangerous. Lucy closed her restive hands together in front of her, for the first time admitting how much she hated the necessity of pretending to be her sister. But Joaquin had personally ensured that telling the truth was out of the question when he had all but threatened to tell Cindy's bridegroom what she was really like. At least what *he* thought her sister was really like, which would be a very biased and cruelly unjust report!

'The remainder could be repaid in instalments,' Lucy proffered a second time, standing her ground and squaring her slight shoulders.

'At Fidelio's age, such an arrangement would not be viable.'

'But I can *prove* that it was all a horrible misunderstanding and that there was no intent to cheat anyone out of anything!' Lucy exclaimed, thrusting up her chin. 'If I had known that Fidelio was working as a ranch foreman, why would I have been under the impression that he was wealthy enough to give away large amounts of cash?'

'Specious,' Joaquin styled that argument, a sardonic ebony brow elevating at her persistence. 'Naturally Mario must have told you that my father had left Fidelio a legacy in his will.'

Lucy paled as she finally understood *how* Fidelio Paez had amassed such a healthy sum for his retirement years. He had inherited the greater part of it from Joaquin's late father, which no doubt gave Joaquin an even more personal stake in the affair. His family resources had ensured the comfort of the older man's retirement, only for Cindy to take it away. But her sister had been guilty of selfish and opportunistic greed, *not* of fraud! There was a distinction and he had to be made to see it. Cindy would not having knowingly injured Mario's father.

'But Mario never mentioned that legacy!' Lucy argued, curling her taut fingers into fists. 'You seem to forget that Mario and...' She stumbled, as she had almost slipped and said her sister's name. 'Mario and *I*,' she stressed, 'were only together for a very short time.'

'Not even long enough for you to play the grieving widow,' Joaquin agreed, studying her with immovable calm.

'If that's another one of those nasty cryptic remarks angled at making me uncomfortable, I'm not listening!' Lucy shot at him in shaken reproach.

'Start facing the fact that I know you for the con-artist you are,' Joaquin countered with unblemished cool, letting his brilliant green eyes roam with insolent thoroughness over her small stiff figure.

Beneath that appraisal Lucy squirmed, with an awareness of his raw masculinity that filled her with furious self-loathing. She could feel the heat rising in her cheeks and the sudden dryness of her mouth but she couldn't afford to stop focusing on the subject at hand. 'You don't know what you're talking about—'

'Don't I? The pre-Raphaelite hairstyle, the big dark blue eyes and the schoolgirl blushes must go down well with men who only see what they want to see...a cute little porcelain doll, the very image of fragile femininity!' Joaquin specified with silken derision. 'But I'm in a rather different league, *querida*.'

'How *dare* you compare me to a doll?' Lucy launched at him with angry incredulity at such a scornful image. 'I came in here to have a perfectly sensible and serious conversation with you—'

Joaquin lounged back against his desk with fluid grace and continued to survey her. 'Did you *really*? Is that why you're all dressed up in that short skirt, those towering heels, and wearing only a jacket next to your beautiful bare skin?'

Lucy ran out of breath and speech simultaneously. She stared at him, totally thrown by that sudden attack of her appearance.

'I'm enjoying the view. I'm a man...' Joaquin trailed out the last word with sardonic cool. 'Yet I've already warned you that I'll accept the invitation but that I won't *pay* for the privilege. I will not settle your debt to Fidelio Paez for you.'

Lucy was engaged in frantically unbuttoning her jacket to display the fine camisole she wore beneath, but then she remembered that she wasn't wearing a bra and just as hurriedly began to button herself up again.

'Oh, not *another* one of those sudden attacks of unconvincing modesty when you blush and lower your eyes and lock your knees together?' the Guatemalan tycoon delivered with withering scorn. 'You're dealing with a true cynic, and let's face it, there was nothing subtle about your visit to my bedroom last night. That was a pretty crude, up-front offer—'

'If you don't shut up, I'll swing for you!' Lucy suddenly exploded back at him, goaded beyond bearing into finally losing her temper. 'You just don't listen to one word that I say. You just won't stop making inappropriate personal comments—'

'On a scale of one to ten, lying on my bed under me is at least a *nine* in the personal stakes. Leaving me aching for the rest of the night made the chances of you attaining a sympathetic hearing this morning doubtful to say the least.'

Oh, how could he say that right to her face? How could he be so *graphic*? Lucy was startled to find herself actually looking wildly around herself for something to hit him with! Freezing to the spot then, she crammed shaking hands to her mouth, appalled by the promptings he roused in her. 'You make me feel violent!' she gasped accusingly.

'I'm not a patient man. Your pathetic attempts to portray yourself as being as pure as driven snow are beginning to irritate me,' Joaquin responded without remorse.

'I-Irritate you?' Lucy stammered, at what struck her as a grotesque understatement for his feelings when it was obvious to her that he utterly despised her. Her looks, her clothing, her character. And somehow accepting that reality emptied her of anger and fight and only pride kept her backbone straight.

'So far I have been very reasonable—'

'Reasonable?' Lucy spluttered. She felt like someone who had been ground into the dust by a large unstoppable truck and then asked to apologise for getting in the way. 'You won't agree to any sort of compromise, even though

I'm willing to repay the money in instalments and do whatever it takes to reassure you as to my reliability—'

'Reliability?' Crystalline green eyes widened and shimmered over her in rampant disbelief at her use of that particular word to describe herself. '*Infierno!* What sort of a fool do you think I am? At this moment you don't even have employment on which to base such promises!'

Once again Lucy cursed her lack of foresight in appreciating just how much Joaquin knew about her sister. Cindy's well paid but temporary contract to work as a television make-up artist had indeed ended, just a few weeks back. But her sister had been promised permanent employment as soon as a vacancy arose.

'In fact over the past five years you have spent only *eight* months actually working for a salary,' Joaquin Del Castillo informed her with considerable contempt. 'I cherish serious doubts that you have *any* ambition to subject yourself to the rigours of daily employment. You're lazy and you're frivolous. If you can find a man to keep you, you don't bother to work—'

Listening to that assessment, Lucy was outraged. 'That's rubbish. I'm a really hard worker, and if I *had* a job, I could make you eat every prejudiced word!'

A charged silence fell.

Her spine rigid with offended pride, Lucy tilted her chin.

Joaquin cast her a glittering glance from below lush black lashes. 'When would you like to start?'

CHAPTER FIVE

'START?' Lucy questioned blankly. 'Start what?'

'Working for me,' Joaquin Del Castillo drawled in challenge. 'What talents do you have beyond the bedroom door?'

Lucy's soft mouth opened and shut again.

'I seem to vaguely recall that you once spent a few weeks toiling as a typist,' Joaquin murmured reflectively, studying her transfixed expression with cynical amusement.

But he had misunderstood the reason for Lucy's absolute paralysis. A typist? He knew more than she did about her twin! No such skill featured in Lucy's repertoire. Nor could she get her mind round the enormous shock of him suggesting that she work for him in any capacity. 'You're...you're offering me a job?' she virtually whispered.

'So that you can make me eat my prejudiced words and prove how reliable you can be,' Joaquin supplied softly. 'Although I'm afraid I couldn't offer you the meteoric rise to promotion which you enjoyed the last time you worked in an office...'

Lucy frowned. 'I don't follow.'

'What a selective memory you have, *querida*. After mere days in the typing pool, the managing director made you his secretary. By the following week you were out of the office and a married man's mistress once more.'

In angry mortification Lucy parted her lips, thought about arguing, clashed with Joaquin's shimmering jade-green gaze and thought better of it. What was the point of getting into another dispute? Right now, although it galled her to

75

admit it, *he* had the whiphand. So she gave a jerky shrug, striving to look untouched and indifferent, just as she knew Cindy would have done under such fire.

Joaquin straightened slowly. 'This is the moment where you tell me that you're still feeling far too fragile to work.'

Meeting his expectant gaze and reacting to it, Lucy flung back her head and snapped defiantly, 'I'm feeling terrific!'

Striding past her, Joaquin flung wide the door with an air of strong satisfaction. 'Then I have the perfect position for you—'

'*Here?*' Lucy stressed with a frown of incomprehension.

Planting a lean hand on her shoulder, Joaquin Del Castillo guided her out into the corridor. Before she could even think, he had shown her through the door at the foot of the passage into a spacious office furnished with what looked to her like the latest in high-tech work stations. 'I maintain only a small staff at here. These ladies handle my personal correspondence and co-ordinate various projects in which I am involved.'

Three female heads lifted. Lucy froze.

Joaquin spoke in Spanish to the older woman who had come forward to greet him. 'This is my secretary, Dominga...Dominga, this is Lucy Paez.'

Lucy received a frigid nod of acknowledgement from the stern Dominga. Like a schoolgirl dragged up in front of the headmistress for some wrongdoing, she quailed inside herself. One glance was sufficient to warn her that Joaquin's secretary knew all about her supposed career as a heartless fraudster. Oh, dear heaven, what had her foolish attempt to defend herself plunged her into now? Joaquin was calling her bluff by offering her the chance to work for him.

'Dominga will keep you occupied,' Joaquin informed her with a slow smile that told her that he had already picked up on the level of her discomfiture.

What followed over the next few hours was one of the most mortifying experiences of Lucy's life.

Cold the older woman might be, but Lucy could not have faulted her fairness. However, finding work to occupy Lucy was not easy. She could not answer the phone or organise documents because she could neither speak nor read Spanish. She had never had access to a computer before either. Asked to fill up the printers with paper, Lucy put the wrong paper in one and provoked a paper jam in the other. Not a woman to give up easily on a challenge, Dominga then went to the trouble of having a typewriter brought in and installed while Lucy hovered, pale as death, unable to muster sufficient courage to admit that she couldn't type.

But the moment of awful revelation was not long in coming. Joaquin's secretary stood like a stone image watching Lucy's desperate two-fingered attempts to pass herself off as a rotten typist but nevertheless a typist. Then the older woman just left her to her foolish charade while the other two women laughed and whispered to each other until Lucy was the colour of a beetroot.

The lunchtime break could not come soon enough for Lucy. Her back aching, she rose from the now hated typewriter and approached the older woman. 'I'm sorry for wasting so much of your time,' Lucy murmured guiltily.

Informed that she might as well take the afternoon off, Lucy turned away, assuming that that was a polite way of telling her not to bother coming back. Her relief was intense. But Dominga then went on to tell her that she would receive basic instruction on how to use a computer the following morning.

Lucy departed, feeling anything but grateful for that offer. Her pride had been hurt by the poor showing she had already made and she was afraid that further embarrassment now awaited her. But then what had she expected? she

asked herself ruefully. Her job at the library had been un-
skilled. She had stamped books, packed shelves and occasionally assisted people to find a particular volume. More
demanding responsibilities had been the province of staff
with degree qualifications. Offered the chance to do evening study, which would have enabled her to apply for a
better position, she had had to refuse because she couldn't
attend the classes.

As she crossed the magnificent hall towards the staircase,
Joaquin strode in through the front doors. He had obviously
been out riding. Sheathed in a crisp white polo shirt, beige
jodhpurs and gleaming dark brown leather boots, he took
Lucy's breath away. 'Drop-dead gorgeous' might have
been a phrase specially coined just for Joaquin Del
Castillo's benefit. The shirt outlined his wide shoulders,
muscular chest and taut flat stomach. The jodhpurs accentuated every sleek line of his long powerful thighs and narrow hips. His black hair was ruffled, his jade-green eyes
brilliant as jewels beneath his level brows.

Her heartbeat went crazy. He was just so beautiful, so
vibrant. He moved with the prowling grace of a jungle cat.
He also emanated a level of high-octane energy which fascinated her. And when he looked at her she felt dizzy, excited, weak at the knees with a wild pent-up anticipation
she couldn't control. He signalled her with a fluid movement of one imperious hand.

It was a moment of revelation for Lucy. It was the moment she admitted that in all her life no man had ever made
her feel the way he did, and that very probably no other
man ever would. She had started falling for him when she
was ill, had learned to look for him then, had felt more
secure when he was around. Trust…was that when she had
given her trust? For, most ironically, she *did* trust Joaquin
Del Castillo.

He might be a serious threat to the happiness of the sister

she adored, but she respected the strong sense of ethics which drove him. How many wealthy powerful men would have taken the time and the trouble to establish why a former employee had decided to keep on working beyond retirement? And how many would have then attempted to right the wrong which had been done?

'Lucy...' Joaquin breathed, his accent very thick.

His crystalline gaze dazzled her. She stilled, and a split second later, his mouth claimed hers in hungry possession. She did not know who moved first. It didn't matter. Nothing mattered but that the awesomely necessary physical connection was made. Her heart thumping like a pounding drum, she clung to his shoulders as he crushed her closer. With the hard heat of his lean, powerful physique welded to her smaller, softer frame, she trembled violently, excitement surging through her like a dangerous drug.

Joaquin freed her mouth and dragged in a jagged breath. He stared down at her with brilliant eyes. 'The *next* time I won't let you go, *querida*.'

Only slowly returning to an awareness of her surroundings, and literally reeling on her feet in the aftermath of that embrace, Lucy drew back from him, stiff as the doll he had labelled her in her efforts to reclaim some composure. 'We—'

His nostrils flared 'There is no "we",' he cut in with ruthless cool.

The heady colour in her cheeks ebbed. 'Of course not...I know that.' But her voice rose in pitch on that admission, a slight quiver betraying her flagging control. She turned away in a rather uncoordinated circle, struggling to get a grip on both her flailing emotions and her treacherous body, which had let her down in the most revealing way of all.

'Have you finished playing at being a typist?' Joaquin enquired smoothly.

'Yes…' Lucy mumbled as she headed for the stairs as if her life depended on getting there.

'I thought you were going to make me eat my words…'

A humourless laugh escaped Lucy. 'Why bother?'

'Sign that agreement. We both *know* that you can afford to reimburse Fidelio,' Joaquin drawled in a tone of derision. 'I'll have you back at the airport within the hour…'

Lucy shut her eyes so tight that they ached. Rigid-backed, she mounted the stairs. Afraid that she was being watched, she didn't dare quicken her steps until she knew herself to be out of sight. Then she hurtled down the corridor and into her bedroom to fling herself in a heap on the bed.

Was it true? Was it true that Cindy had sufficient funds to immediately reimburse Fidelio Paez? Lucy didn't think so. Lucy couldn't credit that her twin could have that much money stashed away. Then the tears she had hoped to hold back by concentrating on that more practical question simply overflowed. Furious at her own weakness, she stuffed her face into the pillows and cried.

She was all worked up, and over what? So she was powerfully attracted to Joaquin Del Castillo, and was savaged by the nasty reality that *he* couldn't wait to get rid of her! Was it her reaction to him which was creating the problem? Or was he just one of those guys who was over-sexed and would make a pass at any reasonable-looking female? Face it, Lucy, a little voice said drily, he's out of your league anyway, and he wouldn't be looking at you twice if there was any competition.

She was already so sick and tired of pretending to be Cindy. Every natural sense prompted her to tell the truth, but intelligence warned her that Joaquin would be even more outraged by the deliberate deception she and her sister had practised. There was no easy way out—no way she could turn something bad into something even acceptable.

The minute Joaquin found that the real Cindy Paez was still in London, he would swing into vengeful action. What might he do in the heat of the moment? She shivered. Cindy did not deserve to have her life wrecked a second time. Lucy would protect her sister for as long as she could while Cindy decided how she was going to handle the situation with Roger.

The arrival of a maid with a lunch tray wakened Lucy up out of the doze she had slid into so easily. She ate with appetite and then decided to go out for a walk. Discarding her twin's now crumpled suit, she donned a floral chiffon skirt. She ignored the long fancy jacket the skirt was supposed to be worn with and teamed it instead with the gypsy top and canvas shoes which she had worn on her arrival at Hacienda de Oro.

Walking out through the front doors minutes later, Lucy breathed in deep in the golden sunshine, delighted to be back in the fresh air. She soon discovered that the lush, informal gardens which contained some incredibly beautiful flowering trees were as spectacular as the views across the deep valley. In the distance she could see the top of an old building showing above the tree canopy, and she began to move in the direction of the forest that ringed the grounds of the house.

A ancient-looking paved lane wound through the trees and Lucy followed it. It was late afternoon by then, and very, very hot, but the further she explored, the more entranced she became. Wildly colourful birds wheeled and dipped overhead, uttering shrill and strange cries. A monkey swung across an overhanging branch, startling her. She laughed as she watched the bright-eyed little creature perch on a tree nearby to study her with patent curiosity. It was like no other world she had ever seen.

Calmer now that she had had the chance to reflect, she saw that she had taken entirely the wrong attitude towards

the office job which Joaquin had so facetiously offered her.
Naturally he didn't expect her to stay the course! And it
was for that very reason that she should stick it out until
he got tired of having her around. If she couldn't prove that
she was reliable, how could she expect him to believe any
promise she might make about repaying Fidelio's money?
A half-hearted approach allied to ineptitude was scarcely
the way to impress a male who already thought she was
lazy and frivolous! So tomorrow she would make a real
effort with the computer training.

That decision made, Lucy rounded another bend on the
worn path she was following. There she faltered to a startled halt, violet eyes opening very wide. Only now did she
recall Yolanda's comment about the Hacienda de Oro being
an archaeologist's dream destination. Before her in a vast
clearing stretched a seemingly endless expanse of Mayan
ruins. The roofcomb of a temple was what she had
glimpsed above the trees from the grounds of the house.

Lucy had always had been interested in the ancient
world. Had she gone to university, she would have studied
archaeology. Then, five years earlier, Cindy had sent her
mother and her sister a casual postcard announcing her marriage to a Guatemalan citizen. Deafening silence had followed until her twin had contacted them again just eleven
months ago. For years Lucy had fondly imagined that her
long-lost sister was living in Guatemala with her husband.
So she had had a special interest in reading about the
astounding ruined cities of the Maya which were sprinkled
across Central America.

She was thrilled to see the extensive and well-maintained
site stretching before her. Before she left London, she had
rather guiltily wondered if she would get an opportunity to
visit one of the famous sites in the Petén, but had deemed
it unlikely when she had believed she was travelling out to
spend her time comforting a dying man. And yet now, here

on the very doorstep as it were, lay the ultimate experience for a keen amateur archaeologist...

Some timeless period later, wholly absorbed in examining in stone what she had previously only studied on a printed page, Lucy's wandering exploration was finally disturbed.

'What the hell have you been doing all this time?' A familiar accented drawl shot at her from a good twenty feet away.

Not having heard Joaquin's approach, Lucy jumped and whirled round in shock. Joaquin was poised by a giant stone stela, surveying her with apparent outrage.

'Sorry...?' As always, he looked staggeringly handsome, and with a feeling of embarrassed self-loathing Lucy tore her gaze from him again. She didn't want to see him. She didn't want to think about him either. Uppermost in her memory was a recollection of her own distress earlier. 'There is no "we",' Joaquin had said drily. He should not have needed to state the obvious. He might not be averse to the inviting signals she could not help putting out in his direction, but essentially Joaquin Del Castillo despised her!

'Armed guards patrol these ruins twenty-four hours a day to protect them. Suppose you had been mistaken for a looter? Where are your wits? You can't just wander off into the jungle as if you're strolling down an English country lane!' Joaquin thundered at her, jade-green eyes glittering with dark fury.

'I'm not in the jungle—'

'You're in the rainforest, you stupid fool!' Joaquin launched at her on full throttle, making her flinch where she stood. 'Have you any idea how long it has taken me to find you?'

'But I wasn't lost...I just followed the path!' Lucy wondered why he looked as if he was just getting more furious

with every word she spoke, and then, realising that she was
staring at him again, she flushed miserably.

Joaquin snatched in an obvious breath of restraint, a feverish line of colour demarcating his fabulous cheekbones.
He punched out a number on the mobile phone gripped in
one lean hand and spoke into it in urgent Spanish. Then he
studied her afresh. 'We've been worried about you! You
left the *hacienda* over three hours ago.'

Three hours ago? People worrying? In dismay, Lucy
checked her watch. 'Oh, my goodness, I'm so sorry…I had
no idea I'd been out here so long!'

'Stop playing it cool. I'm not fooled,' Joaquin delivered
with withering derision. 'You were *lost.*'

'No…' But Lucy looked back in the direction she had
come, only to find that she was no longer so sure of that
direction. She might well have had some difficulty finding
her way back to the path, she conceded grudgingly.

'And since I cannot believe that Mayan civilisation is an
overwhelming passion of yours—'

'I'd just like to see the temple before I leave…'
Screening him out with obstinate determination, Lucy focused on the massive elaborate building which she had
been steadily working towards but continually tempted
away from. 'Please, just give me five minutes.'

'Lucy…'

Since it seemed pretty obvious that she was unlikely to
get the chance of a return visit, Lucy closed her ears and
hurried off.

'Just who are you trying to impress here? Have you even
the slightest conception of what you're looking at?' Joaquin
demanded crushingly.

From the steps, Lucy was engaged in studying the vast
weathered masks of deities adorning the huge ornate entrance.

'Well, that's Hun Hunapu, the maize god…and that one

is—I think—Chac, the god of rain...and this one's Kinich Ahau, the sun god,' she replied self-consciously, and then passed on into the dim interior. 'And I bet I'm mispronouncing those names, because I've only read them and never heard anyone say them out loud. Does this temple have a *pib na*?'

In the incredibly charged silence which followed, Lucy chewed her lower lip and glanced at Joaquin. A deep frownline between his level dark brows, he was studying her with fixed intensity.

'Is there something wrong?' she asked.

Joaquin breathed in deep. '*Sí*...the temple has an underground room.'

'With murals?' Lucy prompted, and then she sighed. 'I suppose the humidity has wrecked them?'

'Not quite...' Joaquin continued to scrutinise her with brilliant green eyes while giving out the impression of a male having a rare struggle to concentrate. 'But while the conservation project is underway to preserve them they are not available for viewing.'

The silence lay heavy between them. Joaquin was very still. Lucy stole a questioning glance up at his lean strong face.

His aggressive jawline squaring, he met her eyes levelly. 'On one count I have wronged you, and for that I owe you a sincere apology. Only out of respect for your late husband's memory could you have taken such an interest in the Maya.'

His sincerity was patent. But that apology hit Lucy like a slap. The colour drained from her cheeks. Joaquin believed he was addressing Mario's widow and he was finally showing some respect. Only he had naturally misinterpreted the connection which had first fired her fascination with the Maya. Suddenly she felt desperately ashamed of the deception she was engaged in.

'It's getting late,' she said stiffly.

But Joaquin rested a light staying hand on her arm. 'You must have loved Mario very much—'

Her discomfiture increasing, Lucy tugged free and started down the steps again. 'It's not something I want to talk about.'

'Perhaps not, but when we were children Mario and I were close friends.'

'I'm sure that didn't last long,' she heard herself snipe, because she was so keen for him to change the subject. 'The heir to the Del Castillo fortune and the ranch foreman's son?'

'It was never like that between us,' Joaquin responded in a quiet tone of rebuke. 'Mario still thought enough of that bond to call me on your wedding day and confess that he was happier than he had ever hoped to be in this life.'

That was an admission which Lucy knew she would pass on to her twin when the timing was right. Only at that particular moment she did not want to be drawn into Joaquin's recollections of his childhood playmate. With every honest word he spoke her own subterfuge made her feel like the lowest of the low.

Joaquin caught her hand in his. 'Look at me...' he urged. 'I pride myself on my judgement, but perhaps I was too quick to judge you for failing my standards after Mario's death.'

'It was a long time ago,' Lucy cut in dismissively.

'*Por Dios!* At least give me credit for finally trying to comprehend what might have made you behave in such an unseemly fashion within weeks of the funeral!'

Lucy yanked her fingers free of his. At that demand, her discomfiture blazed up into angry resentment. 'You patronising bastard...' she whispered in furious reproach.

'*Que pasa?*' Joaquin demanded, his lean darkly handsome features clenching hard on that unexpected attack.

'You…you're wrong about everything!' Lucy flung at him in impassioned defence of the sister she loved. 'And you're far too spoilt to be capable of understanding.'

'Spoilt?' Joaquin repeated in ringing disbelief.

'How many houses does one man need to live in? How could you ever know what it's like to be poor and depressed and not care about anything any more?' she asked in blunt condemnation. 'What would *you* know about the kind of terrible grief that sends people off the rails?'

After that outburst, which had truly come from the heart, Lucy flung him a final look of disgust and took off. He shouted in her wake. Lucy ignored him, which wasn't difficult when he was calling after her in Spanish. In any case she could see the path now and could see no reason to put up with his company when she could find her own way back to the house.

As she sped down the path, she was recalling the evening that her twin had talked about Mario's sudden heart attack. Cindy had confided that she had felt so devastated and wretched after Mario died that she had done some things she had since regretted. Lucy hadn't pried but she guessed she knew what those things had been now. Stripping off for the camera, getting involved with married men. Men who ought to have had more decency, for Cindy could only have been seventeen at the time!

Emerging from her troubled thoughts, Lucy noticed that the vegetation surrounding her seemed much more dense than she had noticed earlier. Exotic plants flourished in a fantastic lush carpet below the trees. Huge ferns, spiky bromeliads and pale orchids shone in the dim, misty light. Yes, the light was fading, or possibly the tree canopy was heavier at this point, she reasoned, and then she heard the sound of rushing water.

She stilled in astonishment at the sight of the waterfall tumbling down over a jutting outcrop of limestone rock into a wide glistening tranquil pool below. The water was so clear she could see each individual pebble below the surface. It was very beautiful. But she was obviously *not* on the same path she had used before.

Joaquin was going to kill her, she conceded ruefully. Bending down, she dipped a finger into the water. It was deliciously cool. Slowly, she raised herself again. She listened to the silence. Even the birds had gone quiet. She was so hot that her damp clothes were sticking to her skin, and getting mad at Joaquin hadn't helped. Just a quick two-minute dip, she decided, succumbing to temptation. Then she would retrace her steps, for goodness knows where she would end up if she stayed on the path she was on!

Peeling off her skirt and top with a sigh of relief, she stepped into the pool. *Heavenly.* She scooped up water and splashed herself all over, revelling in every sparkling water droplet that cooled her overheated flesh.

'Freeze, Lucy...'

Joaquin's drawl was so much quieter than its wont, and such an unwelcome shock, that for a split second she *did* freeze with appalled chagrin, her lack of clothing her most overriding concern. Automatically her head then jerked up and she began to whip her hands over her bare breasts, and then what she saw in that one mortified upward glance filled her with absolute terror...

CHAPTER SIX

IN THE deep shadow below the trees, no longer screened by the thick vegetation, stood the most huge and terrifying beast Lucy had ever seen outside a zoo.

The jaguar was barely fifteen feet away on the other side of the pool. His big golden eyes were drilling holes into her and her mouth fell open. So intense was her fear that she could neither draw breath nor remove her shattered gaze from the animal. And then, with a sudden movement that scared the living daylights out of her and provoked a startled gasp from her straining lungs, the great muscular cat sprang through the trees and was gone.

'Oh, my heaven...oh, my...oh, *my*!' Lucy spluttered through chattering teeth, her near nudity now the very last thing on her mind.

A pair of powerful arms lifted her out of the water and brought her back on to dry land. Trembling violently with fear, she couldn't have spoken to save her life.

'You know the Maya believed that when night fell the sun turned into a jaguar that prowled the underworld,' Joaquin murmured as he peeled off his shirt and dropped it round her shaking shoulders.

'They also called it "the beast that kills its prey with one b-bound"!' Lucy stammered sickly.

'They are rarely aggressive towards humans.'

'Thank the good Lord that he didn't fancy getting those big paws wet!' she gabbled, clutching at a bare broad male shoulder to keep herself upright.

'He is an excellent swimmer, *querida*. This is the pool where he catches fish. You were trespassing.'

89

'Get clothes on,' Lucy mumbled, not keen to hear any further revelations of the big cat's habits.

Joaquin crouched down to gather up her discarded garments. She crouched down with him, pale as death and still shaking like a leaf. 'I was scared—'

'That's good, *querida*. That's more sensible than skinny-dipping in a rainforest when twilight falls.'

'Never again,' Lucy promised in a wobbly voice.

In a deft movement, Joaquin dropped the gypsy top over her head and freed her from his shirt. 'But in all my vast experience I do not think that I ever saw anything as lovely as you were in that brief instant before I saw that you had attracted another admirer.'

With complete calm, he then began inserting her arms into the sleeves of her top while she knelt on the ground in front of him, still virtually paralysed by shock. 'Lovely?' she queried unevenly.

'You...exquisite...your breasts, your hair, the way the light fell on your skin...'

'Oh...' Lucy collided unwarily with shimmering green eyes, conscious of a soaring wicked response she could no more have prevented than she could have denied herself air to breathe. She moistened her dry lips.

'No...' Joaquin decreed in a low-pitched undertone, as if she had spoken.

Only she didn't need to speak to know what he was talking about, and it gave her the most extraordinary sense of power to note the slight tremor in his lean brown hands as he extended them to help her back to her feet. He proceeded to feed her shaky lower limbs into her skirt. She recognised his dexterity without surprise and was amazed by her own lack of concern at being dressed by him. She tried to picture how she must have looked to him in the pool. Clad in nothing but a pair of panties that were wet and probably transparent.

'Did I look sexy?' she heard herself whisper with help-less curiosity.

Joaquin closed big hands over her shoulders and flexed his fingers. 'Like a water nymph in an old painting.'

A water nymph was next door to a wholesome cherub in Lucy's mind. He urged her back the way she had come. Her legs felt ridiculously wobbly. Time itself felt dislo-cated. Traversing the periphery of the ruins, Joaquin turned into the original path where a big four-wheel drive now sat parked. He lifted her into the front seat, hands steady now, and impersonal. As he reversed the vehicle she studied his bold bronzed profile in the dusk light, her heartbeat ham-mering out a dangerous tattoo. In all her life she had never wanted so badly to touch anyone as she wanted to touch him.

When had they stopped talking? When had the silence fallen and the tension begun to build? She didn't know, only that she was awesomely aware of that crackling ten-sion and of *him*. He flipped on the air-conditioning, the click sounding preternaturally loud. He turned towards her, dense spiky lashes screening his gaze to a glimmer of the purest jade. Her fingertips curled in on themselves as she fought the crazy, shameless need to reach out to him.

In the rushing silence she noted everything about him. The faint sheen on his high proud cheekbones, the powerful lure of those bright eyes, the roughened darkness of his uncompromisingly male jawline in contrast to his beauti-fully modelled mouth. A tiny pulse was flickering like mad at the base of her throat as she let her head fall back and just looked at him.

'You like to flirt with danger, *querida*,' Joaquin com-mented, his accent rough as sandpaper gliding over silk.

Never before, probably never again, her rational mind responded. She was dizzy with the tension that held her wire-taut, outrageously aware of the heavy fullness of her breasts and the tiny little twisting sensation curling in the pit of her stomach. He looked and she burned and she melted. It was that simple, that basic, and way too potent a force for her to control. It both thrilled and terrified her to feel the magnetic pull of that power he had over her.

'It's not fair to blame me...' she muttered, dry-mouthed.

Joaquin lifted a lean hand and rested a fingertip against the pulse fluttering wildly at her collarbone. 'No...' he conceded, drawing out the word huskily. 'Desire is rarely so immediate as it is between us. That intrigues me, but it won't hold me. Don't fantasise about a future beyond tomorrow...'

Lucy heard what he was saying and she understood, but she couldn't think about it. She let the words sink unmourned into her subconscious, her whole being concentrated on the mesmeric brilliance of his eyes, the delicious, utterly electrifying sensuality of that light and confident finger now tracing the full curve of her lower lip.

'I've never felt like this before,' she whispered breathlessly.

He cupped her cheekbone, watched her curve her face instinctively into his palm. 'Only teenagers talk like that, Lucy,' he censured with lazy mockery.

'Maybe...' she framed, sealing up the pain of that putdown as soon as she felt it, stowing it away with his words earlier, banishing all that she could not deal with.

'You want me...I want you,' he countered. 'Sexual hunger needs no other label.'

Releasing her then, he turned back to the steering wheel and drove off. She was all of a quiver, intoxicated with longing. She closed her eyes but she couldn't bear it. She had to look at him again. *Sexual hunger?* Not a label she liked. She pushed that knowledge away hurriedly, afraid to face it.

Darkness had fallen at bewildering speed. In the path of

the headlights, Lucy watched him shoot the car to a halt in a courtyard which she assumed lay to the rear of the house. He sprang out and strode round the bonnet. Opening the passenger door, he just scooped her out into his arms.

A shaken laugh escaped Lucy as Joaquin lifted her high in a wholly unexpected manoeuvre that reminded her just how volatile he could be and also deprived her of her shoes, for they fell off. Simultaneously, she noticed that the lights burning in a couple of the ground-floor windows had mysteriously dimmed since their arrival, possibly to allow any staff looking out a better view of what was happening outside.

'My shoes…Joaquin, put me down, *please*,' she urged, hot-cheeked.

'Not until we hit the bedroom.'

'But what about Yolanda?' she gasped, distinctly taken aback by that open avowal of intent.

'My sister has gone to Guatemala city to stay the night with her cousins,' Joaquin imparted. 'Retail therapy will hopefully improve her temper.'

'Retail therapy?'

'Shopping,' Joaquin rephrased, in some surprise that the explanation was necessary.

He swept through a door off the courtyard to mount a back staircase while still holding her as if she weighed no more than a child. He paused on the lofty landing above to claim her lips in a slow, sensual kiss that she found totally electrifying.

Hot and breathless in the aftermath, Lucy opened eyes she didn't remember closing and found herself spread across Joaquin's imposing bed. Her critical faculties were not working at speed and her entire attention was absorbed by the fact that Joaquin had just finished extracting her from her skirt. As she sat up in some confusion, for matters were moving faster than she had naively expected, Joaquin settled crystalline green eyes full of intent on her and peeled off his shirt.

'Oh…' Lucy gasped.

'Oh…what?' The most glorious smile she had ever seen curved Joaquin's mouth.

She was just dazzled by that smile. Heart going nineteen to the dozen, she rested back on her elbows and just stared at him. Shorn of his shirt, he was magnificent. Bronzed skin, black hair, whipcord muscles. As he embarked on his chino trousers she could feel her face hotting up, but she could not resist her own curiosity when that lithe powerful physique was being revealed inch by tantalising inch.

She focused on his washboard-flat stomach and the tantalising silky furrow of hair arrowing down to disappear below his waistband. Then her scrutiny strayed lower and she blinked, jolted out of her voyeuristic reverie. The potent thrust of his arousal was patent. Enervated by the sight, and suddenly desperately self-conscious, she jerked her head away and stared a hole in the door instead.

Nervous as a kitten now, she sat forward, hands linking together. Curiosity had certainly been satisfied. Long past time too, she told herself urgently. Here she was, pushing twenty-three and a virgin. She loved him. He might not love her, but if she chose to overlook the fact that was her business, wasn't it? But if being in a bedroom just watching Joaquin remove his clothes struck her as being the ultimate in intimacy, how was she going to handle what followed? Oh *no*, she thought, gripped by sudden panic, suppose he realised that she wasn't the experienced lover he thought she was?

'Joaquin…?' she began tautly.

'Getting impatient?' Joaquin teased in his dark deep drawl.

'Well…er, no—'

He came down on the bed beside her and separated her

hands so that he could divest her of her top. The operation was so slick she started talking again, only to discover that what she was saying was being muffled by the fabric.

'Cómo?' Joaquin prompted with a frown.

Lucy tugged the gypsy top from him before he could dispose of it and ventured, 'Maybe we shouldn't be rushing into this—'

'Do you feel rushed?' Joaquin rested his hands lightly on her slight shoulders and very gently eased her back against the pillows. 'You are very tense, querida.'

'Yes, but…b-but…'

'I love your mouth,' Joaquin confessed as he leant over her, his breath fanning her cheek, his proximity sentencing her to stillness.

She stared up into his burnished eyes. He lowered his arrogant dark head and very gently brushed her lips with his. 'Oh…'

'You were saying?'

'Nothing…' Engaged on stroking her fingers through his hair, Lucy blinked and turned her mouth up under his in a move so instinctive she didn't even have to think about it.

With a sexy sound, low in his throat, Joaquin pulled her under him and tasted her parted lips hungrily with his own. The concept of escape had evaporated from her mind. As he crushed her into contact with every angle of his over-poweringly male body, she was in more danger of expiring from over-excitement. Her pulses were racing. With the achingly familiar scent of him in her nostrils, every sense she possessed went into overdrive.

He lifted his head and whisked away the crumpled top which still lay between them. His hand curved over the small pouting mounds of her breasts and she quivered, heat curling in her pelvis, making her restive.

'I love your breasts too,' Joaquin muttered unevenly as he disposed of her last garment.

He ran an exploring fingertip over a swollen pale pink nipple and then he dropped his head and let his mouth close round that straining peak instead. The hot rush of physical pleasure took her by storm. She jerked, her whole body trembling. Her skin felt super-sensitive, the force of her own response shocking her, but there wasn't time to dwell on that discovery. His erotic appreciation of her tender flesh was utterly absorbing—until her rising need demanded more.

'Please...' she moaned then.

Eyes glittering, Joaquin surveyed her and let a relaxed hand skim down a taut thigh. Her muscles contracted. She reached up to him, possessed of a fever she barely understood but which nonetheless controlled her. The forceful kiss he claimed only partially eased her nagging tension.

'So you really *do* want me...' Joaquin husked, hauling her even closer with glittering eyes full of conquest.

'Don't you know that?' She gave him a bemused look.

'Women are better liars than men.' He studied her with slumbrous satisfaction. 'But if you had tried to fake your response I would have known it, *gatita*.'

He smoothed a possessive hand over her quivering length. He let his tongue delve between her reddened lips, stoked the hunger she couldn't hide with a carnal level of expertise that she could not resist. As he traced the hot thrumming centre of her body, she arched her spine, a sob of response escaping her convulsed throat. The pleasure became so intense she writhed, driven mindless by her own lack of control.

And then, when she was at the stage when she might have pleaded could she have found her voice, Joaquin came over her, settling between her thighs. 'You're so small, I'm afraid I'll hurt you, *querida*,' he complained raggedly.

Duly forewarned, she still retained enough brain power to react and tense. 'Joaquin?' she gasped.

'*Cristo*…I *know*,' he groaned feelingly, scanning her with glittering eyes filled with need. 'I can't wait any longer either. Never have I been so hot for a woman as I am for you!'

In an instant, the incipient panic she was fighting vanished. Lucy had a vision of herself as the kind of woman who drove a man crazy with desire. She loved that vision. He moved against her. She closed her eyes, and then he was there and it was the most extraordinarily intense moment. Her whole being was centred on that alien intrusion, the sharp stab of momentary pain which made her grit her teeth, but then, caught up in returning excitement, she stopped thinking and started just feeling again.

'You feel incredible, *gatita*,' Joaquin groaned, driving deeper inside her, provoking the most awesomely pleasurable sensations.

From that point on she was lost in her own stormy response. Heart thumping, breath catching, she was caught up in the wild passion he generated. With every smooth rhythmic thrust, he drove her hunger for him higher. She was burning, reaching for the mindless peak of ultimate fulfilment. And then she was there, plunged into ecstasy, crying out in surprise at the height of that pleasure before slowly sinking down to planet earth again.

In the aftermath, she studied Joaquin with wondering eyes. She remembered him shuddering with a driven growl of raw release and she quivered, cocooned in a feeling of decided smugness as she curved up against his big damp body and kissed his shoulder. She was awash with sunny feelings and satisfaction and appreciation.

'You're wonderful,' she whispered dreamily.

'It was good…' Joaquin purred like an indolent jungle cat above her head, accepting the compliment as his due with complete cool. 'In fact, it was spectacular, *gatita*.'

He rolled over, carrying her with him. Then he rearranged her on top of him. He looked down at her, smoothed her tumbled curls back from her brow and slowly eased her back up level with him again to study her with almost frowning fascination. 'I want you all over again.'

'*Sí*...' Lucy said, suddenly feeling confident enough to tease him.

A heartbreaking smile curved Joaquin's beautiful mouth and he relaxed even more. 'And again,' he confided with a husky laugh. 'And again. How many repeat encounters am I allowed?'

She blushed, and pushed her happy face into a broad brown shoulder. 'Who's counting?' she whispered shyly.

He kicked back the sheet. Then he frowned and sat up. She followed the path of his gaze and froze in dismay and chagrin, for there was a small bloodstain on the sheet.

'*Por Dios*...' Joaquin exclaimed.

Thinking faster than she had ever thought in her life, Lucy muttered, 'My knee...I fell when I was scrambling round the ruins this afternoon—'

'And you said nothing?' Joaquin broke in censoriously. 'In this climate, *any* injury needs attention!'

Her scraped knee was duly inspected. Joaquin sprang out of bed, insisting that the cut ought to be bathed and treated with antiseptic. While he occupied himself at that praiseworthy endeavour, Lucy began breathing more normally again.

'You're so careless of your own well-being!' Joaquin's concern was liberally laced with exasperation. 'Even a small wound can lead to a serious infection, and if it's bled again, it hasn't yet begun to heal.'

Lucy withstood the lecture, giddy relief seeping through her as she realised just how close she had come to having her fake identity exposed. Had Joaquin realised that he had been her first lover, he would have known that she could not be Cindy Paez. Joaquin affixed a plaster to the offend-

ing limb and surveyed her where she sat, head humbly
bowed.

'Under no circumstances will you enter the rainforest
again,' he decreed. Her taut mouth began to stretch into a
helpless smile. She stole a glance up at him, irrepressible
dimples indenting her cheeks.

'What's so funny?'

'You're just so bossy. Were you born domineering or
did you get that way growing up?'

Joaquin reached out and very slowly tipped her back
across the tumbled bed. 'The talent comes entirely naturally
to me, *querida*,' he countered with immense cool.

Lucy laughed; she couldn't help it. Joaquin pinned her
hands to the sheet in mock annoyance, his brilliant eyes
intent on her animated face. The leap of instant awareness
she experienced made her still. He smiled again, the indolent sensual smile of a male sure of his welcome, and
bent his tousled dark head to kiss her.

Lucy turned over and reached out, only to discover that she
was in bed alone.

Sitting up, she studied her surroundings in surprise.
While she'd slept, Joaquin must have returned her to her
own room. Discreet and sensible, she conceded, but she
was uneasily aware that discretion had not been on his mind
when he had first swept her off to bed. Suppressing a faint
pang of anxiety, and refusing to acknowledge her disappointment at not waking up in his arms, Lucy got up.

As she showered, all she could think about was Joaquin.
How could she have fallen so much in love in the space of
a week? But then it had been a strange, intense and very
eventful week, and Joaquin was really quite unique. As she
donned a navy shift dress she was recalling her last memories of the previous night. It had still been dark the last
time he had made love to her. His passionate urgency had

set her on fire but burned her out. She had slept, and that must have been when he'd shifted her back to her own bed.

A yawn crept up on Lucy. But, tired as she was, she was determined to show up for the computer training which Dominga had mentioned. She didn't want Joaquin to think that she would try to take advantage of their new intimacy. It was ironic, she thought ruefully. It wasn't for her sister's benefit alone that she was now keen to prove that she was neither lazy nor unreliable.

Hopeful of running into Joaquin, Lucy went downstairs in search of breakfast. However, a maid showed her into a grand and imposing dining room where she found herself eating in splendid isolation. The bubbly sense of happiness she was containing was entirely new to her. She didn't want to examine how she was feeling too closely. She didn't want to let other more threatening thoughts intrude. *He doesn't even know who you are*, an unwelcome little voice whispered regardless at the back of her mind. In panic, she squashed the reminder and closed it out.

Dominga wasn't quite quick enough to hide her surprise at Lucy's arrival. Evidently the older woman had not expected her to show up for work again. She had definitely been seen with Joaquin in the courtyard the night before. How many of the staff suspected that she had spent the night in his bedroom? Lucy paled at those all too realistic concerns and hurriedly shelved them. Somewhere in the back of her mind she was painfully aware that she had broken every rule she had ever respected, but the intoxicating happiness which filled her whenever she thought about Joaquin was far more powerful.

A young male whizzkid arrived to give her the basic training she had been promised on the computer. But Lucy found it incredibly hard to concentrate. Should she have sought Joaquin out before breakfast? Or would that have seemed too pushy? Was she supposed to wait until he came looking for her?

Late morning, Joaquin finally put in an appearance by coming in to speak to his secretary. The instant he entered Lucy's heartbeat speeded up. She almost rose from her seat before she recalled that they had an audience. Feeling bound to stay where she was and allow him to make the first move, she pinned her gaze to his tall powerful figure. His dark grey business suit was superbly tailored to his athletic frame but very formal. For perhaps the first time Lucy recognised *who* Joaquin Del Castillo was. He was a powerful and wealthy industrialist, light years distant from her in status, and finally facing that reality dismayed her.

But, just as quickly, Lucy recovered her confidence. She remembered Joaquin laughing with her the night before, hugging her close with the easy physical affection that was so natural to him and so powerfully appealing to her, and she lifted her head high again.

She waited for him to finish speaking to Dominga. The seconds passed, her tension steadily climbing. His bold bronzed profile looked remote and serious. She wanted to see his eyes. She was just desperate to meet his eyes. But it didn't happen. A moment later Joaquin had strolled back out again without so much as a glance or nod in her direction.

Lucy sagged. He hadn't seen her...of course, he hadn't seen her! She was barely visible seated behind the computer monitor, she told herself ruefully. He might even think she was still in bed. He wouldn't ignore her, would he? Could that be his idea of being discreet? Sort of *super-super-discreet*?

Tortured by such uncertainty, Lucy found that the lunch break seemed to be a long time in coming. But, as soon as it did arrive, Lucy headed straight up the corridor towards Joaquin's office. However, several yards from the ajar door of his office, she realised Yolanda was back; the girl was shouting at the top of her voice. She paused, winced at the chilling timbre of Joaquin's no doubt withering response.

Just as she was about to move on and abandon any attempts to see him, the door flew back on its hinges and Yolanda stalked out, slamming the door shut behind her again. Her stunning face was flushed and streaked with tears. 'I might as well be a *slave*!' she gasped on the back of a distraught sob. 'Joaquin's threatening to take my allowance away. Even my money is not my own. I feel so humiliated!'

'Oh, Yolanda, please don't get so upset...' Without hesitation, Lucy closed a comforting arm round the weeping brunette's waist, which was about as high she could comfortably reach. 'I'm sure he doesn't mean it—'

'Then you don't know my brother,' the brunette whispered raggedly. 'He says that it is his *right* to tell me how to live my life and that I have had too much freedom—'

'Too much?' Lucy was surprised, for on the face of it it didn't seem to her that Joaquin's sister had any freedom at all. Except perhaps in the matter of her fairly noticeable wardrobe.

'Now I am to go nowhere without a chaperon,' Yolanda shared with shuddering mortification. 'At my age! I'll be a laughing stock!'

As the brunette pinned her quivering lips together and turned away, Lucy's heart went out to her. A *chaperon*? In this century? Lucy wasn't surprised the other woman was distraught. Even allowing for cultural differences, Joaquin was treating his sister like a wayward child who had to be kept down and controlled. It was natural for Yolanda fight for independence.

Her brow furrowing on that straying thought, Lucy knocked on the door of Joaquin's office. When there was no response, she went in. Joaquin was standing with his

back to the door. Even his well-cut jacket couldn't conceal
the powerful tension etched into his broad shoulders. As
she entered, he swung round, blazing anger in his shimmering green eyes.

Intimidated, Lucy stilled and watched his darkly handsome features freeze, his brilliant eyes narrow and shutter.

'How may I help you?' Joaquin drawled flatly.

That distant invitation, which carried not a shred of intimacy, made Lucy's cheeks burn as if she had been guilty
of some awful *faux pas*. 'Maybe this isn't the best moment
to…well, er—'

'Why wouldn't it be the best moment?' Joaquin enquired
even more coolly.

Lucy worried at her lower lip, nervous perspiration
dampening her skin. She was so tense her muscles ached.
Suddenly her attempt to see him seemed like a dreadfully
forward move and the ultimate in mistakes. 'I know that
you and Yolanda have just had a bit of an argument,' she
admitted awkwardly.

'That is no concern of yours,' Joaquin countered with
chilling reserve.

'Of course not, but…' Lucy's voice petered out; she honestly didn't know what to say. This was not the passionate
teasing male who had held her in his arms and made love
to her only hours earlier.

The silence lay like a dead weight between them.

'You thought sharing my bed last night gives you some
special privileges?' Joaquin enquired with smooth derision,
an ebony brow slanting.

Every scrap of colour drained from Lucy's face. That
contemptuous question hit her squarely where it hurt. In the
same moment she lost her naive faith in what she had believed they had shared and she was badly shaken. She felt
her knees tremble, her tummy perform a sick somersault.

'Well, possibly one special privilege,' Lucy framed with

strained dignity as she backed towards the door. 'That you would have the good manners not to throw that in my face!'

Suddenly Joaquin unfroze and strode forward to intercept her. 'Lucy…' he grated.

She didn't want to look at him, but she couldn't stop looking at him. Shock was trammelling through her in stricken waves. A faint line of colour accentuated the taut slant of his superb cheekbones. His lean strong face was all angles and tension, a tiny muscle pulling at the corner of his sensual mouth. He had partially lifted one brown hand as though he intended to touch her, but he dropped it back to his side.

'This situation is untenable,' he murmured with harsh clarity. 'Stop playing games, Lucy. Accept defeat, sign that agreement and go back to London.'

'But I—'

'*Por Dios*…I will not conduct an affair with you while my sister is under the same roof,' Joaquin stated with distaste, his strong jawline squaring. 'Last night was complete madness!'

She saw that too now. All of a sudden it was clear as crystal. Surely only temporary insanity could have convinced her otherwise? And it added a whole new dimension to her suffering to appreciate that he had reached that decision long before she had. Without another word, for she wasn't capable of saying anything more, she walked out of his office again.

CHAPTER SEVEN

LUCY found herself back in her bedroom without any recollection of having actually taken herself upstairs.

She lowered herself shakily into a chair and stared into
space. She had behaved like a idiot, she decided. Joaquin
had called their intimacy complete madness, but he didn't
know the half of it, did he? Joaquin still believed she was
Cindy Paez, heartless fraudster and goodtime girl. She
plunged upright again, suddenly desperate to reclaim her
own reputation, her *own* identity by telling him the truth.
Then shame and reason reclaimed her and she dropped back
into the chair again to cover her face with her hands in a
gesture of frustration.

She had promised that she would protect Cindy. She had
promised that she would not betray her. Cindy needed time
to sort out her finances and time to work out how and when
she would tell Roger about the fix she was in. Lucy had
promised her twin that breathing space. In any case, only
a fool would imagine that Joaquin would greet a confession
to the deception Lucy and her twin had engaged in with
anything other than even greater outrage and disgust.

Whichever way Lucy looked at the situation, she saw
that her boats had been burnt the very first day she had met
Joaquin Del Castillo and allowed him to believe that she
was Mario Paez's widow. Since the moment she had met
Joaquin she had been lying her stupid head off! Tough luck
that she had then fallen head over heels in love with him.
But she needn't kid herself that Joaquin would find her any
more attractive as Lucy Fabian. In thinking along that line

she was being pathetic and trying to avoid the real issue, which was…

Joaquin had *dumped* her.

Joaquin had *ditched* her.

Joaquin had *rejected* her.

The fantasy world she had allowed herself to live in for the past eighteen hours had, as a result, just collapsed round her ears. She had been a one-night stand. Not even one full night, she reflected in even greater mortification. He had tossed her out of his bed before dawn and now he wanted her out of his house *and* his country as well. A man couldn't make his feelings much clearer than that!

She had brought it all on herself too! Had she imagined that sex would be the magic way to Joaquin's heart? She cringed, bitterly angry at her own weakness. All the regret that she felt she should have experienced earlier in the day now filled her. She had allowed Joaquin Del Castillo to use her for an evening of entertainment. But how did she blame him when she had virtually offered herself on a plate? It wasn't as if he had even pretended that he wanted a real relationship or anything like that. No one single lie had he told her. And yet *still* she had gone to bed with him! How was she ever going to come to terms with that humiliating truth?

A maid knocked and entered with an envelope.

Rising to reach for it, Lucy turned it over and frowned, registering that it had not come through the post. Only when she had opened it did she realise what it was. The wretched repayment agreement which Joaquin had first faced her with in Fidelio's tumbledown home! What the heck was she supposed to do with it when she *couldn't* sign it?

She had to phone her sister again: she had no other choice. Leaving her bedroom, she just walked straight across the corridor. The door of a guestroom opposite her

own was lying wide, clearly in the process of being aired.
Lucy dialled Cindy's London apartment.

'I thought you weren't going to ring again!' Her twin
gasped accusingly.

'Have you spoken to Roger yet?' Lucy frowned momentarily as she was distracted by a loud click on the line.

'How am I supposed to do that when he's in Germany?'
Cindy demanded.

Lucy had totally forgotten that fact. Only now did she
remember her sister complaining about the fact that Roger's
firm was sending him to Berlin for a fortnight and that he
wouldn't be back until just before their wedding. 'Sorry,
I—'

'Look, there's been a cash offer of the asking price on
your flat and I've accepted it. I intend to tell Roger that
I'm giving *you* the money.'

Lucy tensed in disbelief at the news. 'But—'

'When really I'll be transfering the funds to Fidelio's
bank in Guatemala. OK? Are you satisfied now?'

'You need to tell Roger the truth, Cindy,' Lucy protested.

'No, I don't,' Cindy snapped angrily. 'All *you* have to
do now is convince Del Castillo that that is *all* I can afford
to repay.'

'I don't think Joaquin will accept that.'

'How can you be such a wimp when I'm depending on
you?' Cindy condemned. 'In fact, it strikes me that you've
already made one hell of a mess of things out there!'

Lucy paled, her stomach knotting. 'I've done everything
I could, Cindy—'

'Everything but tell her where to get off!' The unexpected intervention of another female voice on the line gave
Lucy such a shock that she dropped the receiver as if she
had been burnt by it. Yolanda?

Lucy looked on aghast as Joaquin's sister strolled into
the room, cool as a cucumber. She had a cordless phone

clamped to her ear, a phone which she was still actually talking into. 'You've got some nerve, Cindy Paez…sending Lucy over here like the sacrificial lamb, so that you can save your own precious skin!'

'Yolanda?' Lucy gasped, grabbing for the receiver she had dropped to see if her twin was still on the line. *'Cindy?'*

'Who…was…that?' Cindy mumbled, sounding as aghast as Lucy felt.

Across the room the brunette made a production out of lowering her phone to show that she had said all she intended to say.

'Never mind,' Lucy said shakily. 'Bye, Cindy.'

'Let's go for a walk,' Yolanda suggested with an amused look, as if discovering that Lucy was an imposter was of no serious importance.

In a daze, Lucy followed her downstairs. Yolanda walked into a magnificent drawing room, closed the door and settled herself down on an antique sofa.

'How did you find out?' Lucy fixed strained eyes on her companion and stayed upright.

'Easy-peasy. Before you came back upstairs I went into your bag, dug out your passport and *looked*! Then I checked your travel wallet and found this sweet mini photo album. Inside it there's a picture of twin baby girls, and another of you and your sister as grown-ups.' Yolanda rolled her eyes with decided scorn over such sentimentality.

'So now you're going to tell your brother—'

'*Not* necessarily…'

Lucy blinked and focused with widened eyes on the young Guatemalan woman. 'But—'

Yolanda shrugged. 'Joaquin's sure to find out eventually. Why should I get involved? Why should I be the one to blow the whistle?'

Lucy breathed in deep, thinking fast. Right now, Yolanda was at daggers drawn with her brother. Did it give the volatile brunette a kick to know that she had found out the truth about Lucy while *he* was still in the dark?

'I mean one way or another your silly sister will end up paying, because Joaquin doesn't quit.'

'Cindy's not silly...she's just *scared*!' Seeing Yolanda stiffen at that contradiction, Lucy sighed. 'All right, let me tell you the whole story, and then maybe you'll understand.'

Yolanda listened with keen interest, but demonstrated not the slightest sympathy for Cindy's plight. 'I still don't see why *you* should be taking the heat for *her*.'

'Cindy didn't plan it that way.'

'But she's anything but sorry that it's turned out that way!' Yolanda scanned Lucy's troubled face and shook her head in apparent wonderment. 'You're just too nice to fight your own corner. You let everybody walk all over you.'

'No, I don't—'

'What am I doing right now? You didn't even shout at me for going through your handbag!'

Lucy gave her a rueful smile, thinking that for all her sophistication and self-confidence the other woman could occasionally sound very naive. 'I've got more important things to worry about.'

'No, you just need a fast-track escape from Joaquin and I can give it to you,' Yolanda announced.

Incredulity at that announcement blossomed in Lucy's eyes.

Her beautiful companion reddened. 'Well, what's the use of you staying on here? You can't sign that agreement and you can't leave without help.'

'But you're Joaquin's sister,' Lucy heard herself mutter helplessly.

'Half-sister,' Yolanda qualified, tossing her head, her full mouth compressing. 'I'm not being disloyal; I'm just suit-

ing myself. Big Bro will be on your sister's tracks no matter
what happens, and there's nothing you can do about that.'

There was an awful truth to that assurance and it made
Lucy shiver. She could only hope that that bank transfer of
cash which her twin had mentioned would be sufficient to
put Joaquin Del Castillo in a more reasonable frame of
mind where Fidelio Paez was concerned. But she still could
not understand why Yolanda should be offering to help her.

'How would it suit *you* to help me to leave?' Lucy asked
with wide eyes.

'That's my affair. But you have only a few hours to make
up your mind. Joaquin's leaving for a business meeting in
New York later this afternoon, but he'll back by tomorrow
night. I certainly couldn't help you to vanish while he's
still around!'

Joaquin's half-sister rose and glided with fluid steps back
to the door. 'So it's up to you, Lucy. Seems to me you
haven't got many options, because if you *don't* decide to
go I will probably feel that I have to tell Joaquin that he's
got the nice twin instead of the nasty one!'

Lucy's tummy clenched at that unashamed threat. She
hurried to the door, but Yolanda was already heading back
upstairs. It was clear that as far as the brunette was concerned the interview was at an end. So what *was* Lucy
going to do?

Not knowing whether she was on her head or her heels,
she wandered back down to the office. As the staff were
taking the long lunch break favoured in hot climates, it was
empty. She sat down at her workstation and drew in a deep
breath, trying to calm herself down. If she didn't sign that
repayment agreement Joaquin would get really, really furious, and Lucy felt that she had already made enough of
a fool of herself without being forced to hang around where
she most definitely was *not* wanted.

At the same time, however, if she performed a vanishing

act without signing she might well bring down Joaquin on
Cindy's head before the wedding. But wasn't Roger safe
in Germany right now? If she left a letter behind promising
that bank transfer her twin had mentioned, wouldn't that
satisfy Joaquin for a week or two at least? He was a hugely
important and busy guy. How likely was it that he would
drop everything and race over to London immediately?

The door opened. Joaquin stilled on the threshold.

Lucy collided with his spectacular eyes, watched them
narrow and veil. It hurt, it really hurt her to see the cold
distance in his gaze. And right at that minute, when she
herself was aware of him with every fibre of her being, the
pain felt just about unbearable.

'What are you doing in here?' Joaquin demanded with
sardonic bite.

'I didn't feel like lunch—'

'*Por Dios*…you would put up with *anything* sooner than
agree to strip yourself of your ill-gotten gains!' Joaquin
condemned with slashing contempt. 'However, if you're
determined to play this charade out to the bitter end, you
might as well make yourself useful.'

'Useful?'

Joaquin settled a sheet of paper down on the desk beside
her. 'Turn up that file and print it out for me.'

Her teeth plucking at her lower lip as she struggled to
utilise what she had learnt earlier and perform the task,
Lucy found herself wondering why she was bothering. Who
was she trying to impress? Where was her pride? He was
behaving like an absolute louse. She was rigid with the
force of her pent-up emotions. She shifted on the seat, reminded by the intimate ache of her body that Joaquin had
enjoyed a most thorough acquaintance with it before de-
veloping convenient but *very* belated regrets.

'Are you planning to take all day over this one minor
request for output?' Joaquin demanded icily.

Her hands suddenly lifted off the keyboard and balled into fists which she slammed back down on the keyboard again. 'Stop talking to me like that!' she practically shrieked at him as she jumped out of her seat, temper erupting from the emotional turmoil she had been fighting to contain. 'I've got the message...OK?'

'You'll have got the message when you sign that agreement,' Joaquin countered, with a cool that she would have found formidable had she been in a calmer frame of mind.

'For goodness' sake—'

'Once you sign, I may...I just *may* consider calling on you the next time I'm over in London,' Joaquin imparted flatly.

Totally disconcerted by that assurance, Lucy blinked. 'I don't understand—'

'Don't you?' Joaquin vented a cynical laugh, his lean strong features hardening. 'You appeal to the very worst side of my nature, *querida*. If I can contrive to withstand temptation, you won't ever see me again.'

Lucy's soft mouth opened and closed again in slow motion.

Joaquin's jewelled eyes wandered in a leisurely appraisal over her slight slender frame, lingering on the firm swell of her small breasts and the highly feminine curve of waist and hip so well defined by the deceptively simple shift dress she wore. By the time he had completed that increasingly bold evaluation of what they both knew he had an infinitely more intimate acquaintance with, Lucy's cheeks were scarlet and her hands were knotted into defensive fists.

But at that moment it was herself she was fighting rather than him. His potent magnetism was firing the atmosphere between them. That suggestion that he might see her again in London had thrown her, leaving her in no fit state to muster her defences. Her mouth was dry and her heartbeat had accelerated.

Spiky ebony lashes semi-screened his slumbrous green gaze, his beautiful mouth taking on a sensual curve which was all too familiar to her. 'On the other hand,' Joaquin mused in a husky undertone roughened by all-male satisfaction, 'I'm single and I can afford you. Why should I deny myself the occasional indulgence?'

An indulgence? Lucy thought of chocolate as an indulgence, but she had never thought of herself in that line. *I can afford you.* She could not credit that she had sunk low enough to be faced with such an offensive statement. That Joaquin even felt confident enough to say that to her appalled her. Then she met those brilliant knowing eyes of his and she paled to the colour of parchment and finally understood. Joaquin Del Castillo was supremely well aware of his power over her. It was the final humiliation and it chilled her physical response to his presence.

'You think I...you think I care about you,' she said unsteadily.

Joaquin spread fluidly expressive hands in a gesture that was anything but an indication of humility.

'And you are ready to *use* that to make me do what you want?' she framed, in quivering disbelief that any male could be that cruelly manipulative.

Joaquin gave her a measured nod of confirmation.

Lucy folded her arms in a jerky motion. She thought of the way she had behaved the previous night. She was no actress, and had had no idea of playing it cool. She had probably betrayed herself a hundred times over in the way she'd looked at him and what she had both said and done. At the very least, he knew that she was keen. No longer could she meet his eyes. She was deeply shaken by the degrading proposition he was outlining to her.

'I *do* understand your shocked sense of injustice, *querida*,' Joaquin murmured silkily. 'How many times have

you run rings round men crazy for you? But this time
around it's going to be different.'

Lucy stepped out from behind the workstation separating
them, two coins of high colour adorning her taut cheekbones. 'If you think for one moment that I'd be stupid
enough to let you reduce me to the level of some tramp
you spend the night with whenever you feel like it—'

'Such emotive words,' Joaquin sliced in, smooth as glass.
'Yet you set no boundaries last night. You wanted me too
much to be sensible or calculating and it paid dividends, *es
verdad*? For what I am now offering you is an arrangement
to which you are uniquely well suited—'

'No, I'm not!' Lucy gasped in stricken outrage.

Shrugging a wide muscular shoulder in a very Latin dismissal of that protest, Joaquin continued to rest his incisive
green eyes on her angry face. 'In this life we all end up
settling for the best we can get. So choose between me and
the money you conned out of Fidelio. You can have one
but not *both*. And if you choose me, it will be only on my
terms.'

'I just can't believe you're talking like this to me!' Lucy
confessed with raw honesty.

'Isn't it marvellous that you should still possess that en-
dearing little streak of almost child-like innocence when
things don't pan out quite the way you planned them?' A
grim smile flashed across his devastatingly handsome features as he paused by the door. ' No man in his right mind
would keep you in an office, *querida*. When you punched
the keyboard you crashed the whole system. I'll have to
contact my head office in London to get those figures now.'

In a daze, Lucy focused on the monitor, which had gone
all blurry and now bore a large error message. The other
two computer monitors bore similar messages as well.
Momentarily she closed her eyes to get a grip on her seething emotions. But Joaquin had knocked her sideways. He

had a head office of some kind in London? How often *was* he in London? Dismayed by thoughts that should have no place in her head, she experienced a burst of self-loathing. Even if Joaquin Del Castillo was in London every blasted week she would never willingly set eyes on him again! He was so sure of himself, so certain he had her where he wanted her. Well, he would soon find out that she learnt from her mistakes!

Lucy went off in search of Yolanda, and with the assistance of a maid eventually ran her to earth in a custom-built gym where the gorgeous brunette was doing what appeared to be graceful ballet exercises at a bar.

'I've thought over what you've said,' Lucy proclaimed, coming to a breathless halt several feet away. 'I'll take your help...I want to go home!'

As that last phrase emerged, more in the nature of an over-emotional wail, Yolanda stilled to stare at Lucy. 'So Joaquin's been spreading his special variety of joy and happiness in your direction as well.'

'This has got nothing to do with your wretched brother!' Lucy snapped, rather foolishly in the circumstances.

Yolanda's attention had already strayed. Her lustrous brown eyes glowed with satisfaction. 'I'd love to see Joaquin's face when he realises that we've *both* done a vanishing act!'

CHAPTER EIGHT

BY LATE evening of the same day, Lucy had learnt just
how hard and embarrassing it could be to perform a vanishing act in which Yolanda Del Castillo played a leading
role.

Noting with relief that the volatile girl was now asleep,
Lucy subsided back into her own comfortable seat on the
plane. Just an hour into a flight to London, Lucy was counting the cost: her nerves were in shreds and she was exhausted. Yet Yolanda had engineered their departure from
Hacienda De Oro with remarkable efficiency.

While Lucy had sweated blood over the writing of an
explanatory letter to Joaquin concerning the cash transfer
which Cindy had promised for Fidelio, Yolanda's maid had
packed for Lucy and whisked away her suitcase. She had
then been shown down to a rear exit. Outside had sat a
four-wheel drive with Yolanda in the back seat.

'Lucy, hurry up and drive off before we're seen!' she
had urged.

That was when Lucy had discovered why she had been
so essential to Yolanda's plans. Yolanda had seen Lucy's
driving licence in her handbag.

'Of course I do not drive myself,' the brunette had responded when Lucy had voiced her surprise. 'I am always
driven, but if I ask one of the staff to take me to the airport
Joaquin will find out long before I get there!'

Lucy had found that long drive a nightmare. She had
never driven such a huge car before, nor had she had prior
experience of driving on a different side of the road. Then
there had been the horrors of the busy traffic in Guatemala

city, the wrong turns she had made, the cars that had hooted furiously at her. Lucy had been a nervous wreck by the time they'd finally reached the airport. But there had been worse to come...

Even two hours after the event, Lucy just cringed at the memory of the dreadful scene Yolanda had thrown when she'd been told there were no seats left on the flight she wanted to board. She had proclaimed that she was Yolanda Del Castillo at the top of her voice. She had ranted and raved until she'd got what she wanted. She had also insisted that Lucy's economy class ticket be upgraded.

'Joaquin is held in huge regard in my country. They will bump other passengers off the flight for my benefit,' Yolanda had forecast smugly. 'After all, it is a great honour that I, a Del Castillo, should travel on their airline!'

That forecast had proved correct. Then Yolanda had thrown *another* tantrum on boarding, to ensure that they secured the most spacious front seats in the first class section. Two middle-aged businessmen had scuttled into other seats like mice. Worst of all, Lucy had received censorious glances from other passengers, as if they somehow imagined she ought to be cooling Yolanda's outrageous behaviour.

No longer was Lucy surprised that Joaquin had been playing the heavy big brother with his demanding sister. Yolanda was immature—outright uncontrollable if she was crossed—and terrifyingly unscrupulous. More like a nightmare teenager than an adult, Lucy conceded inwardly. Had great wealth and too much indulgence made Yolanda that way? Had Joaquin been trying hard to straighten his sister out?

'I really like you, Lucy,' Yolanda had confided before she'd gone to sleep. 'When I've set up my own apartment in London you can come and visit me if you want.'

Lucy just couldn't understand why she was feeling so

responsible for Yolanda all of a sudden, but it seemed to her that in spite of her stunning looks and seeming sophistication Yolanda was woefully unsuited to the independence and freedom she craved.

With every airborne mile that carried her further from Guatemala and Joaquin, Lucy got more and more miserable. How would Cindy feel about her coming home without having sorted out her twin's problems in the way she had hoped and expected? Joaquin would be even more furious that Lucy had vanished along with his temperamental sister. It just seemed that no matter what she did, she did it wrong...

'I'll call you when I have time,' Yolanda promised as her cases were loaded into the cab which Lucy had procured for her outside Heathrow. 'Don't expect to hear from me *too* soon, though. Socially, I shall be very much in demand.'

Lucy went straight to her sister's apartment. Cindy was stunned to find her on the doorstep, but her first reaction after she overcame her astonishment was to give Lucy a relieved hug. 'Thank goodness you're home! Did you get everything settled?'

'Not quite—'

'You didn't sign that agreement, did you?'

Lucy shook her head and explained the situation she had left behind. While engaged in making a welcome cup of tea for her twin, Cindy listened anxiously and then began to look perplexed.

'Why do you keep on saying his name that way?'

'Whose name?'

'Joaquin...'

Lucy flushed. 'I'm not saying it *any* way. He was just pretty central to events, that's all.'

Her twin refused to be sidetracked. 'Are you telling me

that you went and *fell* for the guy who's trying to wreck my life?'

'With a little bit of luck it won't come to that if you settle this business with Mario's father once and for all.'

'I *will*. I saw a solicitor yesterday and he'll handle it. But right now it's *you* I'm more interested in.'

'I just want to forget I ever went to Guatemala,' Lucy muttered truthfully.

Silence lay for a second or two.

Then Cindy shrugged. 'Well, if Del Castillo comes here looking to cause more trouble, he won't find me. I've been hired by a film unit that starts shooting in Scotland this weekend and I have to be at the studios in another hour!'

'Sounds like fun…' Lucy concealed her disappointment that her twin was leaving almost as soon as she herself arrived.

'But it means I won't be here to help you get your flat packed up. The buyer wants possession as soon as possible. And the sooner he gets in, the sooner Fidelio gets his cash,' Cindy pointed out. 'I haven't decided yet what I'm going to tell Roger.'

'You know…I thought you'd be furious with me for just coming home.'

Cindy grimaced, her colour heightening. 'Yolanda fairly put me in my box with what she said on the phone. Why *should* you take the heat for me? I'm sorry that I got you into this mess in the first place,' she admitted ruefully. 'My sins have come back to haunt me and I'll just have to handle the fall-out as best I can.'

With that one brief and effective little speech, Lucy felt the difference between her twin and her more impressionable and anxious self. Cindy might have panicked when she'd first learnt about Fidelio's predicament and Joaquin's demands, but ultimately Cindy rolled with the punches and took each day as it came.

Thirty minutes later, seated in the cab which would take her back to the flat she had once shared with her mother, Lucy sighed. The crowded city streets and the cold dull winter weather seemed a poor exchange for the lush beauty of a colourful country like Guatemala. But she had her sister's wedding to look forward to, and then Christmas, she reminded herself. Hadn't she always loved the festive season? But Roger and Cindy would still be away on their honeymoon and Christmas would be rather lonely…

Two busy weeks later, Lucy moved into her sister's apartment. Cindy was still not home. Her twin had finished working with the film unit but she was currently in Oxford, staying with Roger's parents, to where he would return from Germany. Their wedding was now only three days away and, thanks to the organisational skills of Cindy's future mother-in-law, her sister had virtually no last-minute details to check.

Within ten minutes of sitting down in her sister's lounge mid-morning, to take a break from unpacking, Lucy fell asleep. When she woke up again, she was exasperated with herself. Why was she so tired all the time? In addition, her tummy was out of sorts and she had had a couple of minor dizzy spells as well.

As she had tried to explain to her doctor forty-eight hours earlier, it wasn't that she felt exactly ill, more that she just didn't feel quite *right*. Had she some infection which she had yet to shake off? Her doctor had done some tests. She was to phone later to get the results, she reminded herself ruefully.

The intercom buzzed as she was making up a bed for herself in the spare room. Walking out to the hall, she caught her reflection in the full-length mirror on the wall. Gosh, she looked drab and washed out! After the experience of wearing her twin's designer garments, she had become uncomfortably aware of how dowdy her own clothing was. Her blue tunic sweater and long skirt might be warm and comfy but they had neither shape nor style.

However, she was stuck with the wardrobe she had. Right now, she was poor as a church mouse, and she had more pressing priorities. Although she had managed to find a temporary job as an assistant in a toy store over the Christmas period, and was starting work the day after the wedding, she still needed to find somewhere of her own to live.

'Yes…?' she said into the intercom.

'Buzz me up…' Joaquin drawled in the most lethally intimidating tone.

Lucy froze. Instant recognition of his dark deep drawl sent her into a mindless tailspin. 'B-but—'

'*Now*, Lucy!' Joaquin thundered without hesitation.

In a total daze, she hit the button. There was just no stopping the soaring sense of joy and excitement washing over her. *He was here in London!* All right, so he didn't sound as if he was in the best of moods, but any minute she was going to see him. She opened the door and turned in a dizzy little circle and then stilled in guilty dismay. What the heck was she thinking of?

Laying eyes on Joaquin Del Castillo again would put her right back to the beginning of the recovery process. Not that she had travelled that far along the road to recovery, she conceded reluctantly. After all, she still thought about Joaquin at least once every five minutes, and in particularly weak moments almost constantly. But, like it or not, Joaquin did not feel the same way about her. So it would be foolish for her to feed her craving for him with further exposure.

Just as she heard the lift doors whirring back on the landing, Lucy went to close the apartment door again.

'Sorry, I just don't think this is a good idea, but you could always phone me—'

Joaquin took her totally aback by forging forward regardless. Thrusting the door wide enough for entrance, he simply lifted her out of his path and set her down again before she could offer any further objection. 'Right, where is Yolanda?' he demanded with raw impatience.

Disconcerted by his aggressive attitude, and flustered by being lifted off her feet like an exasperating but minor obstruction, Lucy just gaped at him. Joaquin looked as if he had been through hell since she had last seen him. His brilliant eyes were shadowed. His stunning cheekbones were sharper and fierce lines of tension bracketed his taut mouth as he studied her with charged expectancy.

Yolanda! Lucy was sharply disappointed and felt that she should have been better prepared for that demand. Naturally he was angry that his sister had left home in defiance of his wishes. And, being Joaquin, an autocrat to his fingertips, he obviously wasn't going to let the matter lie. Even so, Lucy was jolted by the sense of rejection she experienced at the reality that his visit had nothing to do with her personally.

She was very pale. 'I really don't think I can tell you where your sister is without her permission—'

'Either you tell me or you tell the police!' Joaquin shot back at her without hesitation.

'The p-police…?' Lucy repeated in a wobbly burst of incredulity at such a threat.

'I am outraged by your behaviour in this business,' Joaquin informed her, his strong jawline clenching hard. 'How could you help Yolanda to run away from home? She left me a letter telling me that she was returning to school. Fool that I am, I was so relieved that I did not even check her story! Then I waited a week to let the dust settle before I tried to call her.'

Like a woman turned to stone, Lucy mumbled thickly, 'School?'

But Joaquin was still talking. He drove an angry hand through his thick black hair and focused on her with shimmering green eyes full of condemnation. 'When I discovered that she hadn't returned to school I assumed that she was with you. This apartment has been under surveillance ever since then. I have been awaiting your return.'

'*School?*' Lucy said a second time with greater stress as Joaquin strode past her into the lounge. She followed him. 'Why are you talking about Yolanda going back to school?'

'Where else should a sixteen-year-old be?' Joaquin demanded wrathfully.

'A *sixteen*-year-old...she can't be...no, there is no way she can be just sixteen!' Lucy protested, gazing back at him with disbelieving eyes.

'Where the hell *is* she?' Joaquin launched at her again.

Shock and the most appalling feeling of guilt assailed Lucy. The depth of his anxious concern for his sister's welfare was patent. She had been taken in by a teenager playing a role that had come easily to a young girl raised in the lap of luxury and indulgence. Aware that Lucy was impressed by that act, Yolanda had ensured that she stayed fooled. When Lucy had finally got around to asking what age the brunette was on that drive to the airport, Yolanda had lied and said she was twenty-one. But why, when she had actually witnessed the other girl's wilful moods and immaturity, had she not put two and two together and at least *suspected* the truth?

'I honestly didn't know what age she was, Joaquin. Oh, my goodness, what an idiot I've been!' Lucy exclaimed, biting at her lower lip and shaking her head.

Joaquin closed lean hands round her forearms. 'All I need to know right now is *where* my sister is. Much will be forgiven if she is safe and unharmed.'

'She phones me most days.' Lucy dashed the sudden rush of tears from her strained eyes. 'Last week she flew to Paris to visit some friend called Loretta—'

Releasing her, Joaquin produced a portable phone. 'What is Loretta's surname?'

'I don't know, and it hardly matters because Yolanda is back in London again. For goodness' sake, she spent most of yesterday with me!' Lucy confessed. 'She said that she was in a hotel, but she didn't say where and I never thought to ask. She seemed rather lonely, and I would've asked her to stay here with me, but—'

'It might have cramped your style?' Joaquin slotted in with fierce derision.

Lucy paled at that crack. But she could not explain that the apartment was not hers without admitting that she was *not* Cindy Paez, and at that moment there were more important things to worry about. Genuinely agitated by what Joaquin had divulged, and feeling very much to blame, Lucy sank down giddily into an armchair.

'Have you a contact number for Yolanda?' Joaquin shot at her.

'No…she's always called me,' Lucy admitted heavily. 'Joaquin, I *swear* I hadn't a clue how young she was!'

But Joaquin was no longer listening: he was on his phone talking in urgent Spanish. His bold bronzed profile stood out in sharp relief against the pale wall behind him. He moved one hand expressively as he spoke, spreading his long fingers, closing them again while restively pacing the floor. She had forgotten his vibrant energy, the way he seemed to take over and dominate a room the minute he entered it. A tide of tormented awareness which she would have done anything to suppress washed over her.

'What phone number will Yolanda be using to contact you…the one here?' Joaquin swung back to her to demand.

'No…' Lucy breathed in deep to explain, but embarrassed colour now put to flight her previous pallor. 'Yesterday was my birthday and she gave me a mobile phone as a present. She said she was fed up not being able to get hold of me when she wanted me…she hasn't called me on it yet, though.'

'Then, you and your phone can come back to *my* London home with me! *Por Dios*…don't you dare try to argue with me!' Joaquin warned with ruthless bite as her lips parted in dismay. 'I'm not letting you out of my sight until I get my sister back and you are the only lead I have right now!'

Feeling as responsible as she did over a situation which she had helped to create, Lucy got up without argument. 'I'll get changed.'

Joaquin scrutinised her slender taut figure, a deep frown line slowly forming between his dark brows. 'Why are you dressed that way?'

'What way?'

'Like some older woman who doesn't care how she looks any more,' he extended with a questioning slant of an ebony brow.

Lucy edged out of the lounge without responding. Joaquin had finally had the opportunity to see her as she *really* was and he wasn't exactly thrilled by the view. Shorn of her twin's fine feathers, she had lost any claim to glamour. On that galling thought, she hurried into her sister's room. There she picked out a black skirt, a soft turquoise twinset and a pair of high heels. She refused to think about why she was raiding her twin's wardrobe in the midst of a crisis in which her appearance should be the very last thing on her mind.

Joaquin tilted back his arrogant dark head to study her as she made her breathless return, clutching a small travel bag. She could feel her face burning as he appraised the snug fit of fine wool over her breasts and the slim length of leg now on view. Suddenly wishing that the floor would open and swallow her, Lucy turned away. Talk about being obvious! Rushing to put on a more flattering outfit had to have given him a very clear message as to her susceptibility, but to her relief he made no comment as she locked up the apartment.

Out on the street, a limousine awaited them. Lucy settled back into the rich leather upholstery, striving to act as if she travelled in similar style every day.

'You're lucky that I didn't involve the police in this,' Joaquin delivered without warning, throwing her a grim glance that made her back into the furthest corner of the seat. 'My sister is a very rich young woman. Had you not accompanied her back to London, I would have been afraid that she had been kidnapped when she failed to show up at school. But, though I have little faith in your moral principles, I did not believe that you would put Yolanda at risk.'

'For the last time,' Lucy groaned ruefully, 'I didn't realise she was only sixteen!'

'Isn't it strange, though, that in spite of that age-gap the two of you seem to be very much on the same wavelength?' Joaquin drawled in a sardonic aside.

Lucy decided to ignore that crack. 'Is Yolanda's mother over here with you?'

Joaquin vented a cynical laugh. 'No, Beatriz isn't in London. She has no interest in what her teenage daughter does.'

Lucy frowned. 'Why?'

'Beatriz was my father's second wife and very much younger.' Joaquin murmured drily. 'When he died, he made my sister an heiress, but his will decreed that Beatriz would lose much of her income if she remarried.'

'Which she did?'

'Beatriz and her new husband then had the responsibility of handling my sister's trust fund. However, gross financial irregularities persuaded the trustees to make other arrangements when Yolanda was nine years old,' Joaquin explained with sardonic cool. 'When Beatriz was no longer in a position to rob her daughter blind, she chose to send her off to an English boarding school and more or less forget about her.'

Lucy was shaken by that unemotional rendering of unpleasant facts. 'I'd already gathered that she and her mother weren't close, but—'

'Beatriz resented having a daughter so much richer than she was herself.' Joaquin made no attempt to conceal his derision. 'Yet her present husband owns a very large and successful construction company and they are by no means poor.'

'Did you have much contact with Yolanda while she was growing up?'

'Not enough to establish the relationship which her mother was determined to discourage. But when my sister's school suspended her as a punishment—'

Lucy winced. 'What did she do?'

'She sneaked out to a nightclub and got her face splashed all over the tabloids. Where do you think the It Girl fantasy came from?' Joaquin enquired drily. 'Beatriz said she could no longer cope with her and sent her to me. When the suspension was up, Yolanda then refused to return to school.'

'So that's what the arguments were about,' Lucy sighed. 'I got hold of entirely the wrong end of the stick.'

The chauffeur opened the door beside her. Lucy blinked in disconcertion and scrambled out. She had been so involved in her conversation with Joaquin that she hadn't even noticed that the car had drawn to a halt outside an imposing Georgian house in a quiet residential square.

The spacious hall was beautifully furnished and very elegant. A manservant spread open the door of an equally impressive drawing room.

'Where's the phone Yolanda gave you?'

Lucy dug the cerise pink phone out of her bag and extended it.

Joaquin removed it from her hold. 'It's not even switched on!' he shot at her incredulously.

Lucy reddened. 'I haven't read all the instructions yet, but I did charge it—'

Joaquin flicked through the buttons and then set the phone down on the coffee table. 'You haven't missed any calls.'

She took a seat in an armchair. She studied the beautiful wool rug fixedly, felt her stupid eyes sting with tears. How pathetic she had been, rushing to borrow her sister's clothes like an over-excited teenager invited out on a hot date! It was so obvious that there was just nothing there for him any more. But then weren't a lot of men supposed to be like that? She was no mystery now. She was not outstandingly beautiful either. Why, she hadn't even bothered making use of the cosmetics which Cindy had painstakingly taught her to apply! That passionate night at Hacienda De Oro had been a mistake as far as Joaquin was concerned. And now, more than two weeks on? The way *he* was behaving, she might as well have dreamt up the entire encounter.

'You realise that you can't tell Yolanda I'm here when she rings,' Joaquin spelt out.

Lucy nodded.

'That you have to find out where she's staying and arrange either to go over there or to meet up somewhere? I don't want her vanishing again,' Joaquin completed.

Lucy nodded a second time.

Where were her wits? What was going on inside her head? *This* was the guy who had suggested he might call in for the occasional night of recreational sex when he was in London. Suggestions didn't come much more offensive.

In fact, if he was to lay a single finger on her she would scream and tell him exactly where to get off! Only it didn't look as if she was about to get the opportunity to demonstrate her aversion to him.

The manservant reappeared with a tray of coffee. Joaquin moved his hand in a negative motion signifying disinterest. Lucy poured a cup for herself while he paced the floor in preoccupied silence.

'*Infierno!*' Joaquin bit out, half under his breath. 'What the hell am I supposed to say to Yolanda when I *do* get hold of her?'

That driven demand touched Lucy's heart and chipped away at the barriers she was striving to raise for her own protection. She watched him spread his hands and drop them again in an expressive gesture of frustration. In his dark navy pinstriped business suit he looked so cool and elegant and distant, but his crystalline green eyes betrayed the depth of his anxiety.

'I think your sister needs to know that you love and care about her—'

'She *must* know that!'

'I'm not sure she does,' Lucy sighed. 'And try not to be confrontational. If she doesn't want to go back to school, there have to be other options that could at least be discussed.'

Joaquin elevated a derisive ebony brow. 'You want me to sit down with a big smile and tell her she can be a wild child if she wants to be?'

At that crack, Lucy abandoned her coffee and stood up. 'No, just let her know that you're willing to listen. A lot of what Yolanda says is just *talk*. She hasn't even gone to any nightclubs.'

Joaquin raised both hands in an impatient motion of dismissal, his darkly handsome features hard with resolve. 'I know what is best for my sister—'

'You've already admitted that you don't know her very well, so how *can* you know?' Lucy asked him ruefully.

He tensed and lost colour beneath his bronzed complexion, but he didn't lower his arrogant dark head one inch and his brilliant eyes reflected ice-cool scorn for that reminder.

'OK...you asked, and now you're putting me down for answering, but that attitude won't work with Yolanda. She's as stubborn and hot-tempered as you are!' Cut to the bone by that silent derision, Lucy turned away.

His lean hands came down on her rigid shoulders and slowly turned her back. She focused on his smooth gold silk tie. Long fingers curved under her chin to make her look up. 'I'm sorry, *querida*. I've never been very good at taking instruction.'

The sound of that familiar term of endearment closed Lucy's throat over. She gazed up at him, strained eyes wide and wary. 'I was tactless—'

'What you said was right. I've made mistakes...I can't afford to make many more with her...'

He was close, and she was so intent on him that she had already lost the thread of the conversation. Those beautiful eyes of his filled her with such a powerful longing to touch him that she clenched her hands by her sides to keep them there.

'Where have *you* been for the past two weeks?' Joaquin asked levelly.

'I told you in my letter...the flat—the one you said didn't exist,' she framed as a reminder. 'It's sold, but it had to be cleared for the new owner.'

'No such property appeared in the list of your assets.'

Lucy was having a real struggle to concentrate. 'Someone slipped up—'

'So it would seem.' His dark rich drawl seemed to slow

down and lower in timbre, sending a delicious shiver down
her taut spinal cord.

Her lower limbs untrustworthy supports, she trembled.
In the charged silence, her heartbeat had speeded up to a
mile a minute. The fierce tension of her taut muscles made
her all the more aware of the swollen sensitivity of her
breasts and the ungovernable ache building between her
thighs. Nor was she so lost to all reason that she heard no
inner voice urging retreat; she heard it but blanked it out,
for the craving was stronger.

'*Dios mio...*' Joaquin sounded thickly, his fingers wind-
ing into her luxuriant caramel-coloured hair to tug her head
back very gently. His scorching gaze raked over her face.
'Do you know how difficult it was to put you back into
your own bed that morning? I didn't like that...I didn't like
being that hungry, *gatita*. I didn't like aching to have just
one more chance to feel you going wild under me...'

'No?' Her voice was a mere thread, for she was mes-
merized by what he was telling her.

'No,' Joaquin breathed in roughened confirmation. 'Only
a weak man lets desire come between him and reason. But
two weeks has been enough of a deprivation for me to feel
I have more than made my point.'

'You missed me...' Lucy muttered, hanging on his every
word.

'Every hour on the hour...' Joaquin let his hands drop
to her hips, to skim up her skirt and then hoist her up
against him. 'More cold showers than I could bear. But I
know now what it is that draws me. You're like a split
personality, *querida*. I'm fascinated. How could I be anything else?'

Drawn only partially from her sensual abstraction, Lucy
blinked, assuming she had misunderstood. 'A split—?'

Joaquin let his tongue delve between her parted lips with
an erotic expertise and promise that was not best suited to

enabling her to hold up her end of a sensible conversation. She jerked against him, a stifled moan breaking low in her throat as the feverish hunger he had already ignited took fire in excitement.

'Of course, I *know* what you are...I know exactly what you're capable of,' Joaquin murmured against her cheekbone while she was fighting to get back the strength to breathe. 'But you've honed your camouflage skills to the level of an art form.'

'I don't know what you're talking about—'

Both arms banded round her, Joaquin settled fluidly down on to a sofa with her astride him. One hand closing into her hair to tip her head back, he pressed his lips to the delicate skin just below her ear. Suddenly it felt like the most erotic spot in her whole screaming body. She gasped out loud, clutched at his hair, feeling the burn of her own excitement in sensual shock.

'Don't you?' Joaquin prompted almost roughly, framing her flushed cheekbones with both hands and holding her entrapped, scorching green eyes delving into passion-glazed violet-blue. 'You're like a chameleon and you're very clever. You give every man what he wants: in fact you *become* what he wants.'

'Joaquin, I—'

'*Silencio, por favor.*' He rested a warning fingertip against her lips.

'B-but—'

'It's the secret of your success, *querida.*' Joaquin scanned her shaken expression with satisfaction and lowered his hands again. 'Where did you swot up on Mayan ruins to impress me? In my *own* library? That romantic little dip you took in the forest, knowing that I was on your trail—'

'No...you're wrong!' Lucy was appalled by the suggestion that she had planned everything that had happened between them, had indeed waged a campaign to attract him.

'And that night in my bed you gave me the shy but eager virgin that every Latin American male fantasises about. It was an illusion, *naturally*, but it was a brilliant performance,' Joaquin assured her appreciatively as he let his sure hands stroke caressingly from her slim hips along the extended length of her taut slender thighs.

The arousing glide of his hands on her over-sensitive flesh made her tremble, but she was taken aback by the rock-solid conviction with which he spoke.

'If I didn't excite you quite so much, you would be white with shock,' Joaquin forecast with galling amusement. 'Did I neglect to mention that you can continue moulding yourself into being exactly what I want with my full support?'

'You're calling me one big fake!' Lucy condemned strickenly, and then she froze on the awareness that *that* was exactly what she was. Fake name, fake appearance, fake everything!

'Big hurt eyes and cue for tears that well up,' Joaquin labelled silkily, throwing his arrogant dark head back to study her with intense concentration while retaining his imprisoning hold on her. 'And, even though I know it's a superb act, I feel like a bastard for hurting your feelings.'

'Let go of me!' Lucy wailed, anchored to his muscular thighs in what now seemed to her to be the most mortifyingly inappropriate position.

'No…' Joaquin told her, taking her soft mouth with a sudden dark passionate force that caught her totally by surprise.

She brought her hands thumping down on his broad shoulders but somehow forgot to coil them into fists. And then that moment of resistance was gone. Her need for him was greater. Within seconds she was kissing him back with the same drugging intensity he was teaching her. Raw seething excitement gripped her. She pressed herself as close as she could get, which wasn't close enough, and with a husky growl Joaquin started rearranging her, an operation complicated by his apparent reluctance to separate from her for a single moment.

'*Por Dios*…you can set me on fire with a kiss, *querida*,' Joaquin breathed raggedly.

Lucy looked up at him, vaguely wondering how they had got to be lying down full length on the sofa, but considerably more aware of how incredibly good it felt to have the heavy masculine weight of him against her again. And then she heard a curious little metallic rendition of what sounded remarkably like the opening to the 'The Teddy Bears' Picnic'…

Just as suddenly, Joaquin thrust himself away from her and vaulted upright. He snatched up the mobile phone and extended it to her with a hand that was noticeably unsteady. 'Yolanda, it must be…make the lies good,' he urged unevenly, dulled colour lying along his taut cheekbones.

But as it turned out Lucy had no need to tell a single lie. Indeed, during the brief conversation which followed she had more trouble getting a word in edgeways. Yolanda had had her purse stolen from her bag in a shop and was in floods of tears. 'I've got no money…what do I do?' she asked brokenly.

'We'll be right there…OK?' Lucy promised soothingly.

On the way back out to the limousine, Joaquin said incredulously, 'You said only *four* words and yet you betrayed my presence—'

'She's far too upset to worry about who "we" stands for,' Lucy muttered shakily, still in shock at her own behaviour—and his. Her wanton body was still all of a quiver. She was desperate to put some distance between herself and Joaquin while she dealt with her emotional turmoil, but she also felt the need to rush to Yolanda's side, because somehow she had become fond of the younger girl.

And Yolanda, touched for the first time in her life by crime, only froze for a split second when she saw her brother approaching a step in Lucy's wake. Although she was relieved to see Lucy, it was self-evident that the arrival of a strong male figure on the scene was even more welcome after the shock the Guatemalan girl had suffered. As bursts of rapid Spanish were exchanged and Yolanda turned instinctively to her bossy big brother for support, Lucy felt very much like a third wheel.

Since there was little hope of its recovery, Joaquin suggested that the stolen purse should be reported to the police immediately, any credit cards cancelled, and that later they would go straight to Yolanda's hotel so that she could pack.

'You can come in with me, Lucy,' the brunette told her more cheerfully.

'I'd like to, but I'm afraid I have an appointment this afternoon,' Lucy responded uncomfortably, still not having met Joaquin's eyes once since they had left his townhouse.

'But I need some company,' Yolanda protested with reproachful eyes.

'Come back to the house with us and join us for dinner,' Joaquin murmured smoothly, adding his voice to his sister's.

'I'm sorry, but I really do need to get home. I'd be grateful if you could just drop me off at the nearest bus stop,' Lucy stated tautly.

After all, Joaquin thought that she was a fake and she *was* a fake—indeed a much bigger fake than he could ever have guessed. He was a clever guy. How could she have been so foolish as to imagine that he would not sense on some level that she was not quite what she appeared to be? And what other interpretation could he have put on behaviour that just didn't match what he believed he knew about her background and lifestyle? After all, her twin *was* very different, in personality and presentation. Cindy was confident, occasionally even aggressive in her outlook on the world, and nobody's fool. Cindy was not shy or awkward or naïve.

It was time that she cut loose of *any* connection with Joaquin and Yolanda Del Castillo, Lucy conceded heavily. Cindy had put a solicitor in charge of any further communications with Joaquin concerning the repayment of her former father-in-law's savings. There was no further need for Lucy to play any role, nor any requirement for Joaquin to be told that she was, in fact, Cindy Paez's sister. In any case, sooner or later his *own* sister would inform him of that fact and probably laugh her head off at how he had been fooled.

As neither Del Castillo was accustomed to having their wishes ignored and their invitations refused, there was a distinct coolness now in the atmosphere.

'I'll call you...' Yolanda said sullenly, when the limo stopped to let Lucy alight. Ironically the brunette finally both looked and sounded her age.

Joaquin flashed Lucy a darkling glance of censure but Lucy evaded it. He would have invited a chimpanzee home for dinner had he believed it would keep his volatile sister happy, she thought bitterly. She caught the bus and went shopping for food. On her walk back to the apartment she found herself passing within yards of her doctor's surgery and decided to call in for her test results in person.

The receptionist checked the card, which had a note attached. 'You need to make another appointment.'

'Another?' Lucy queried anxiously. 'Does that mean something came up in the tests?'

'I expect it's just the norm for a first pregnancy,' the young woman said blithely. 'I'll check with the doctor now. I can never read his handwriting.'

had happened to her confidence, and yet, she didn't have
expected that once in her Joaquin may made love to her
once. But when she finally finished clearing up how many
times Joaquin had ... she felt herself being trapped revealing
of the reality that she had ... lived a child wherever she
domed alive. Had Joaquin or from only so ...

CHAPTER NINE

PREGNANT?

No, there was no doubt, no room for error, Lucy's doctor
had assured her in the five minutes which was all the busy
older man had been able to spare her before his next patient
arrived. Tests were now so advanced that they could pick
up a pregnancy at the very earliest stages, even before the
menstrual cycle was noticeably disrupted. Lucy had stumbled out of his surgery again like an accident victim.

The possibility that she might be pregnant had not even
occurred to Lucy. In retrospect she was shattered by the
realisation that she hadn't once thought of that risk. Not
that night she had been with Joaquin and not afterwards
either. She had never had any reason to think about contraception, having always naively assumed that she would
be in a long-term serious relationship before she became
sexually involved. On the face of it, what *did* that wild
passionate and romantic night of lovemaking with Joaquin
have to do with the production of a little baby nine months
down the line?

Only now the connection between those two events was
painfully obvious to Lucy, and she was deeply ashamed
that she had behaved in such an immature and irresponsible
way. A baby...Joaquin's baby. Not a piece of news she
could picture him greeting with anything other than outrage. But then hadn't Joaquin, with considerably less excuse, been equally careless of consequences? Lucy's bowed
shoulders straightened a little on that conviction. Was she
supposed to believe that a male of his sophistication and
experience had been so overwhelmed with desire that he

had forgotten to use contraception? Well, she might have conceded that excuse had Joaquin only made love to her *once*, but when she finally finished counting up how many times Joaquin had made love to her she stopped marvelling at the reality that she had conceived a child after one abandoned night. Had Joaquin been industriously set on creating a baby, he could not have made more effort to that end!

After a sleepless night, Lucy was tidying the kitchen early the next morning, taking refuge in keeping herself busy in an effort to keep herself calm, when she heard the front door open.

'Lucy...?'

She stiffened in astonishment because it was her future brother-in-law's voice. 'I'm in here, Roger!'

Roger Harkness appeared in the doorway. He was a big, thickset young man, with light brown hair and deceptively bland blue eyes set into lean, sun-tanned features. 'Cindy warned me to shout first in case I gave you a fright.'

'I thought you were staying in Oxford until tomorrow?'

'Cindy and my mother *thought*...and Cindy had to stay because my folks have invited a pile of guests round this evening,' Roger grimaced. 'But my firm didn't send me to Germany for two weeks just to have me roll back last minute, get married and go off on honeymoon without reporting back somewhere in between!'

'It's a shame, though—'

'I have to write up a detailed report and present it first thing tomorrow morning to the senior partners. I'll get it finished quicker here.'

'I didn't move any of your stuff in the spare room,' Lucy hastened to assure him, reminded that the room she was currently occupying was the same one which Roger, having given up his own flat before he went to Germany, had set up as a home office in which he could work.

'I wouldn't have worried about it if you had,' Roger

assured her with a rather strained and unconvincing smile. 'I'm really tired, so I'm going to hit the sack for a couple of hours and then start work.'

As he trod off down to the bedroom, Lucy bit anxiously at her lower lip. The sooner she found herself a bedsit the better. She didn't want to be playing gooseberry to a newly married couple. Even using the spare room she would be inconveniencing them. Roger had seemed tense and awkward with her, unlike his usual genial self.

Poor Cindy, Lucy reflected sympathetically, her thoughts turning to her twin, who had been so much looking forward to her reunion with Roger, only now to find it cut short. Roger had only got back from Germany the night before. He must have driven straight to Oxford, spent the night and got up at dawn to get back into London so early. Certainly her twin wouldn't have had the opportunity to make any serious confessions to Roger. But then *when* her sister chose to tell Roger about the financial hot water she was in was really none of her business, Lucy reminded herself.

Didn't she have enough problems of her own to worry about? Exactly what was she planning to do about the fact that she was pregnant? She wasn't prepared to consider a termination. She would have her baby…Joaquin's baby. No matter how *he* felt about it. But how would she live? It was all very well making airy-fairy plans to raise a child on her own, but Lucy was already foreseeing how difficult it would be.

She wasn't capable of earning a salary big enough to cover the cost of childcare. In some circumstances government help was available to assist single mothers to stay in employment. Only she didn't have a clue whether she would qualify for help, didn't have a clue where she would live, how she would live…*anything*!

And at that point of rising panic, the doorbell went. Rushing to answer it, while being surprised that it hadn't been the intercom which had sounded a warning of a visitor first, but too preoccupied to put on the security chain, she just opened the door.

'Allow me to tell you that the security is useless in this building,' Joaquin informed her with grim disapproval. 'The main entrance door downstairs was lying wide open. Anybody could just walk in!'

But *he* had. And in that first time-suspended moment of recognition Lucy was overwhelmed by happiness. Thought had nothing to do with it; instinct reigned supreme. There he stood, looking breathtakingly, stunningly handsome in a black cashmere overcoat worn over a faultlessly cut dark business suit. But then her brain kicked back into functioning again and she went rigid.

'Joaquin...?' The birth of sheer panic turned Lucy pale enough to make his keen gaze narrow in his inspection of her now startled face. But she couldn't help but be aghast at his arrival. Roger was in the apartment! Roger had never even heard of Joaquin Del Castillo but Joaquin had certainly heard of Roger, and if the two men were to meet and Joaquin learnt how he had been deceived what else might be said in Roger's hearing? If Roger *had* to find out what his bride-to-be and her sister had been doing while he was safely out of reach in Germany, the very worst way he *could* find out would be from a male who had as low an opinion of Cindy as Joaquin had!

'Why are you looking at me like that?' Joaquin strode smoothly past her into the hall.

'Sorry...I wasn't expecting you,' Lucy muttered in a stifled undertone, her shaken appraisal pinned to his tall powerful frame while she tried feverishly to work out how to get rid of him again.

'Are you normally this slow on the uptake in the morning, *querida*?' Joaquin teased with husky amusement as he thrust the door shut behind him.

She was discovering that she could not meet those extraordinary green eyes without being intimately aware that she had conceived his baby. It was bad enough that she was terrified that at any moment Roger might appear to find out who was visiting, but to be burdened with yet another big guilty secret where Joaquin was concerned was all of a sudden just too much for Lucy to handle. Sheer nervous tension made her tummy lurch with nausea.

'Are you ill?' Joaquin began to question with a frowning look of concern.

With a stifled moan of chagrin, Lucy raced for the bathroom, but she had the presence of mind to close and lock the door behind her. She was sick. In the aftermath, the loud thumping on the door demanded her attention.

'Lucy…don't be stupid, open this door!' Joaquin urged with considerable impatience.

Hurriedly freshening up, capable of considering nothing but the reality that she felt absolutely awful, Lucy went dizzily back out to the hall.

'Suppose you'd collapsed in there?' Joaquin curved a supportive arm round her slim shoulders and then with a muttered curse in Spanish lifted her into his powerful arms to carry her into the lounge opposite and lay her down on the sofa. 'I'll get a doctor. You're just not a very healthy person, *querida*. I think you need a really thorough medical examination—'

'No, I—'

'Lie there and keep quiet,' Joaquin instructed, standing over her clutching his mobile phone with an air of serious purpose. 'How could I have taunted you with the amount of time you have spent out of work in recent years? It is obvious to me now that you suffer from a great deal of ill-health.'

'I really don't need a doctor,' Lucy began, trying to sound forceful enough to stop him in his bossy tracks.

'Allow *me* to tell you what you need.'

'But you don't know—'

'I know it's not normal to look green,' Joaquin slotted in crushingly.

'I'm pregnant…' The confession just escaped her in a weary burst of resentful frustration at his refusal to listen to a word she was saying.

But this time Joaquin *had* listened, and the phone dropped clean out of his hand as he involuntarily loosened his grip on it. His lush ebony lashes lifted, revealing stunned green eyes. But then the oddest thing happened. He screened his gaze again, threw back his wide shoulders as if he was squaring up to a challenge, and said only the slightest bit unsteadily, '*Sí*…so you *still* need a doctor.'

'Talk about interrupting…at the optimum wrong moment…' another male voice groaned from across the room.

In all the excitement, Lucy had totally forgotten about Roger. She was still caught up in the drama of having told Joaquin she was pregnant without actually having intended to tell him. But the sound of Roger's apologetic intrusion was an even greater shock, and she reared up off the sofa just in time to see her sister's large bulky fiancé backing speedily into the hall again, looking almost comically embarrassed by what he had overheard.

'*Por Dios*…no wonder you acted so weird when you saw me at your door!' Joaquin framed thickly, his accent growling along every carefully enunciated syllable. His bronzed skin had an ashen quality as he studied her with seething contempt.

'I think…I think it's time that I explained something to you,' Lucy muttered tautly, thinking frantically fast and seeing that full confession was the only option left. 'But could we go somewhere else to talk about it because it's kind of private?'

'Roger Harkness…what need is there of privacy to explain his presence here in your apartment?' Joaquin demanded with volcanic force, spreading both arms wide with the sort of volatile expressive body language that was extremely intimidating. 'You got back into bed with your ex-fiancé after sleeping with me. I neglected to offer you an option sufficient to keep you *out* of other men's beds! You came back here to *him* last night…you slut!'

Lucy turned pale as death. 'It's not like that, Joaquin, because—'

Joaquin focused on her with a dark blistering fury that only seemed to heighten with every second which had passed since Roger's hasty exist. 'And now you're pregnant and you can't possibly know *which* of us is the father…I'll get DNA tests done when the baby's born. In the meantime, he's welcome to you, if he still wants you, but only *after* I've beaten the living daylights out of him!'

For a staggered instant, Lucy was paralysed to the spot by that unashamed threat of violence. Joaquin strode out of the room like a man on a mission. Lucy regained the use of her limbs and surged in his wake. 'Joaquin…for goodness' sake!'

But Joaquin was throwing wide every door he came to in search of a fight, indifferent, it seemed, to Lucy's efforts to prevent him. Nobody was more surprised than Lucy when Roger failed to appear. She reckoned that her future brother-in-law must have walked straight out of the apartment to give her and Joaquin peace to talk.

'*Infierno!*' Baulked of his prey, and incredulous that Roger had evidently just gone out and left them alone together, Joaquin grated in wrathful frustration, 'What sort of coward is he that he runs away from a fight?'

'Please just calm down for a moment and listen to me,' Lucy urged feverishly.

Joaquin turned ferociously bright green eyes full of condemnation on her. 'Listen? Listen so that you can whisper lying explanations into my ears and try to convince me that the child you carry is mine?' he countered with savage derision. 'It will snow in hell before I *listen* to you again!'

And with that highly emotive smouldering condemnation, Joaquin strode out of the apartment.

Lucy was in a sobbing heap on the sofa when Roger reappeared. 'So that was Joaquin Del Castillo,' he remarked as Lucy crammed a tissue to her mouth and sat up, struggling to pull herself together again. 'I feel really sorry for that guy.'

Stunned by that most telling admission from her sister's fiancé, Lucy gaped at him.

'Yes, I know the whole story. Cindy kept me up until dawn talking about it,' Roger revealed. 'I'm more or less beyond being shocked now, but she didn't mention that *other* matter...the one I really would rather not have overheard.'

'Cindy doesn't know and I'm not going to mention it just yet,' Lucy muttered tightly on the subject of her pregnancy. She realised that she was kind of beyond shock as well, after the distressing encounter she had just had with Joaquin. The guy she loved, the father of her baby, had just walked away, thinking all sorts of crazy horrible things about her.

'I want to thank you for looking out for Cindy while I was away,' Roger said flatly. 'I owe you...we both owe you on that score.'

Lucy gave him a blank look.

'Come on, Lucy. Your common sense prevented her from making a bad situation ten times worse. If she'd lost her head and dug her heels in, she most probably would have ended up in court accused of fraud,' Roger stated tautly, his frank open face stiff. 'Quite frankly, it's fortunate it *was* you in Guatemala!'

Lucy was embarrassed. She could see that he was still angry with her sister.

'With my help, Cindy will pay back every penny with interest to that old man,' Roger told her squarely.

'But she didn't *mean* to hurt anybody,' Lucy pointed out hurriedly, before he left the room, still looking really grim.

Her thoughts turning to her own situation then, Lucy accepted that she had got herself into an awful mess. No matter which way she broke the news, Joaquin would be outraged by the manner in which she and her sister had deceived him, and Lucy knew with a sinking heart that she would have to wait until the wedding was over before she risked telling Joaquin the truth of her identity.

Roger's faith in Cindy had been shaken. The very last thing Roger needed now was to see her twin confronted by Joaquin in a righteous rage. That might just be the straw that would break the camel's back. Lucy already suspected that Roger had used this report for his firm as an excuse to put some distance between himself and her twin while he came to terms with what he had been told. What if Roger decided to call off the wedding? Lucy saw for herself that the situation could still go either way. Right now, marooned with Roger's parents, forced to go on pretending that she was a happy bride-to-be and entertain visitors, poor Cindy *had* to be really suffering.

So, although every instinct Lucy possessed was urging her to track Joaquin down without further loss of time and tell him that she was *not* Cindy Paez, she didn't feel that she could dare take that risk in case it rebounded on her twin. But, at the same time, it really hurt Lucy to leave Joaquin believing that she had already turned to another man and that she couldn't be sure of *who* had fathered their child. Right now, Joaquin truly believed that she was a slut. Hadn't she been in his arms yesterday? However, in about

forty-eight hours she could get in touch with him and sort
it all out, she promised herself wretchedly.

In the afternoon, Lucy went out and walked round the
shops, with their wonderful festive displays. Roger had
been pacing restively round the apartment, looking increasingly uncomfortable at her presence. That had worried Lucy
even more. Naturally he would start feeling awkward if he
was toying with the idea of dumping her sister two days
before their wedding.

Yolanda called her on the mobile phone she had given
her. 'Have you still got Joaquin with you?' she asked
brightly.

'No, he's long gone...I mean, he didn't stay long,' Lucy
rephrased hurriedly.

'Did he offer you the job?'

'What job?'

Yolanda proceeded to tell her that she was prepared to
go back to school but only as a day girl, not as a boarder.
Joaquin had pointed out that, although he could spend more
time in London, he was often abroad and she couldn't stay
alone in the townhouse with just the staff for company.

'So I suggested that he could give you the job of being
my companion,' Yolanda completed with satisfaction.

Lucy looked heavenward for inspiration. Even if Joaquin
hadn't received the impression that she was a bed-hopping
wanton earlier in the day, he would not have offered her
such a position. Yolanda's idea had never been destined to
make it off the drawing board.

'Thanks, but it wouldn't have been a good idea for me—'

'Lucy,' Yolanda scolded. 'You're crazy about my
brother and I like you. If he saw enough of you, he might
be attracted to you.'

'I think a little of me goes a long way with Joaquin right
now,' Lucy muttered, not knowing whether to laugh or
to cry.

'Why haven't you told him you're the *other* twin yet?' Yolanda demanded. 'Do you want me to do it for you?'

Lucy paled to the gills at the offer, and felt even worse about what she had to go on to say. 'Please don't do that, Yolanda. I promise I'll tell him in a couple of days. I'm very sorry that I've involved you in keeping a secret from your brother.'

'Get real, Lucy,' Yolanda groaned, sounding her world-weary best. 'Do you think I tell him *everything*?'

Lucy climbed out of the wedding car, clutching her posy of flowers, and followed the other three bridesmaids, composed of Roger's three chattering sisters.

All of them wore beautiful white silk brocade dresses, for Cindy had reversed the more conventional colour choices and chosen a wedding gown that was her favourite shade of pink. They congregated in the big church porch and then surged forward to greet the bridal limousine drawing up. Looking radiant, Cindy emerged and took the arm of Roger's father who had offered to give her away.

'You're too early.' One of the ushers came out to warn them. 'Roger's been held up.'

Cindy went white. 'Where is he?'

'Panicking in a traffic jam!' the usher teased. 'Should be here in five minutes.'

The day before, Lucy had spent a great deal of time trudging round the shops. In the early hours, Cindy had returned to London to mend fences with Roger. Lucy hadn't the slightest idea of what had passed between the couple, but Cindy was still a nervous wreck, convinced that her bridegroom had come close to changing his mind about marrying her.

A long low-slung black sportscar shot to a halt in front of the church steps, where nobody was supposed to park. Lucy saw it first because everybody else in the porch was

too busy talking. With shaken eyes, she watched Joaquin
Del Castillo vault out of the car as if he was jet-propelled,
his darkly handsome features fiercely set.

Having heard the sound of the car, Cindy hurried forward
to her twin's side. 'Is that Roger arriving?' she asked anxiously.

Like somebody just waiting for the roof to fall in on her,
Lucy watched Joaquin heading for the steps. Her heart was
racing so fast she was afraid that she was about to faint. It
seemed that Joaquin had finally found out that she and
Cindy had deceived him. What else could he be doing here?
But how had he found out? Had his sister told him? Was
he now prepared to confront Cindy in front of all these
people on her wedding day...*would* he be that cruel?

'Oh...no,' Cindy whispered in horror, having read her
sister's face. 'That's Del Castillo...isn't it?'

Joaquin mounted the steps two at a time. But he stopped
dead when he saw Lucy, frozen on the top step and looking
almost as pale as her dress. *'Por Dios,'* he exclaimed
hoarsely. 'This cannot be. You cannot do this...I will not
allow it—'

'Please...please go away,' Cindy pleaded tearfully.

Only when Cindy spoke did Joaquin take the time to
glance at the woman who stood by Lucy's side. He frowned
as he focused on Cindy, the look of disbelief in his glittering green eyes instantaneous. He stared at the two sisters.
'Infierno...there are *two* of you?'

It was the longest moment of Lucy's life. 'We're twins,'
she muttered unevenly. 'I'm Lucy—'

'I know you're Lucy!' Joaquin gritted. 'Do you think I'm
so blind I can't tell you apart?'

'I think what my sister is trying to tell you is that I'm
the one who ripped off Fidelio Paez,' Cindy told Joaquin
tightly. 'I'm the one who married Mario and the one who

persuaded Lucy to go to Guatemala in my place and pretend that she was me.'

So intense was Lucy's concentration on Joaquin's stunned stillness she was conscious of nothing else. She couldn't even concentrate on what her sister was telling him.

Cindy just kept on talking, as if by talking she could keep any threat Joaquin might offer at bay. 'Lucy didn't want to do it but I made it very difficult for her to refuse...I took advantage of her—'

Joaquin cut right across her. 'Which one of you is the bride?'

'Me...Cindy,' Cindy responded, in visible bewilderment at such a question.

A dark line of colour flared over Joaquin's fabulous cheekbones. The silence smouldered for what felt like for ever. 'Enjoy your wedding day, Cindy,' he murmured without expression.

Cindy backed away like someone who very badly wanted to pick up her skirts and run but who was afraid that any sudden movement might provoke exactly what she most feared. 'Thank you,' she whispered unevenly.

Only now was it dawning on Lucy that Joaquin had thought that this was *her* wedding day!

'And for your sister, that selfish, frivolous user and abuser of other people, you lied to *me*,' Joaquin breathed in a terrifyingly quiet voice.

The buzz of the chattering bridesmaids in the background might as well have been a million miles away. Lucy's world had stopped spinning and flung her off into frightening freefall when she least expected it. It was as if a pool of rushing silence enfolded her and Joaquin.

'I believed it was *you* who was marrying Roger Harkness today. Your sister's neighbour laughed when he saw me outside the apartment. ''All away to the church,'' he said.'

Joaquin breathed in very deep and studied the pale oval of her stricken face with cold hard eyes. 'I cannot abide lies, and every word you have ever spoken to me has been a lie, every single moment has been based on deceit.'

At that harsh condemnation Lucy made a tiny instinctive movement with her hand, as though she would have touched his sleeve. But Joaquin's distaste and anger was a potent barrier and her hand dropped weakly back to her side.

'No...no, it wasn't,' she attempted to protest.

'I don't even know your name...' Joaquin flung back his proud dark head and surveyed her with speaking contempt.

'Lucille Fabian,' she framed chokily. 'Joaquin, *please*—'

'This is not the place. My presence is not welcome here. Surely you did not sacrifice so much just to cloud your sister's wedding day?' Joaquin said very drily, and he swung on his heel to stride back to his fabulous car.

If Lucy had been in freefall prior to that moment, she now felt as though she had hit the ground with a bone-jarring crash. After an instant of hesitation, Lucy flew down the steps in Joaquin's wake.

'There's Roger's car!' someone exclaimed behind her. 'They're coming in by the side entrance.'

Before Joaquin could get back into the Ferrari, Lucy caught at his sleeve with desperate fingers. 'I'm sorry!'

Ice-cold green eyes clashed with hers. 'You're making an exhibition of us both.'

Lucy fell back from him. A slow, painful surge of pink washed her cheeks. Turning away, she walked back up the steps, horribly conscious that the little drama being played out before their eyes had finally attracted the attention of the rest of the bride's attendants in the porch.

Cindy hurried forward and closed an arm round her twin. 'I'm sorry...I am *so* sorry,' she whispered shakily.

'It wasn't going anywhere anyway,' Lucy framed, trying

to force a smile and relieved when, a few minutes later, the church doors were opened and it was time to get into place with the other bridesmaids.

Joaquin had come to the church believing that *she* was the bride. Had he had some mad idea of preventing the wedding from taking place? 'I will not allow it,' he had said. Well, what did his motivation matter now? She had never been able to believe that her relationship with Joaquin Del Castillo could have a future. But her failure to tell Joaquin the truth the day he saw Roger in the apartment had probably been the finishing blow. Right to the bitter end she had kept loyal to Cindy—but shouldn't she have had a greater sense of responsibility towards the baby she had conceived? Ensuring that Joaquin despised her would scarcely benefit her unborn child.

At the beginning, pretending to be Cindy had been like a game she'd played, she saw now. Exotic travel and fancy clothes had been seductive trappings for a young woman bored with her own dull and uneventful life. Nor could she blame Cindy for persuading her into that disastrous masquerade. Her twin had had no suspicion that Joaquin Del Castillo had sent the plane tickets to snare a woman he believed to be a con-artist.

Yet Joaquin had had right on his side in what he'd been trying to do. She had even recognised that reality. She had tried to persuade herself that she was still lying for her sister's sake, but by then hadn't she been just as afraid that telling Joaquin the truth would wreck any chance she had with him? Not until she had witnessed Joaquin's absolute revulsion had she registered just how inexcusable her continuing deception had become. Like many other people, Joaquin couldn't stand liars. And Lucy had never felt so miserable in her life.

Outside the church after the ceremony, when the photographer had almost finished his task, Roger strolled over to Lucy's side, bent his head and said to her with a grin, 'Have I got a surprise for you!'

Her brow furrowing, she turned to ask her new brother-in-law what he meant, but Roger and Cindy were already heading for the car which would ferry them ahead of their guests to the reception. However, Lucy did not have very long to wait to discover the surprise in store for her. The very first person she saw when she walked into the hotel function room was Joaquin!

Sheathed in the dark suit that fitted his wide-shouldered, slim-hipped physique to perfection, his white shirt and elegant silver-grey silk tie accentuating his bronzed skin and black hair, he looked stunningly handsome. But what shocked Lucy even more was that Joaquin was with Roger, and the two men appeared to be conversing with all the ease and familiarity of old friends.

Breaking away from a group of guests, Cindy made a beeline for her twin. 'When Roger arrived at the church, he saw you outside with Joaquin. He guessed who he was and he jumped out of the car before Joaquin could drive off and persuaded him to come to the reception. Roger trying to play cupid...I still can't believe it!'

'Yes, well...' Lucy was all too well aware of why Roger had made that effort on her behalf. Roger knew that she was carrying Joaquin's baby, news that she still had to share with her sister.

'And Roger didn't even tell me what he'd done until we were on the way here, and now, for goodness' sake, they're getting on like a house on fire!' Cindy marvelled with a rueful but accepting laugh. 'Isn't that just like men? They just ignore all the drama and start talking about sport!'

One of the bridesmaids settled a drink into Lucy's hand. Across the foyer, Joaquin finally took note of Lucy's presence. Brilliant, unreadable green eyes rested on her taut face, and with a final word to Roger he strode over to her.

'Well, this is a surprise,' Lucy began awkwardly.

Joaquin elevated a sardonic brow. 'Is it? Roger stepped into the breach with admirable common sense. Fidelio's problems may be at an end but your brother-in-law knows that ours are *not*. Even if I wanted to, I'm not in a position to just walk away now.'

At that grim assurance, Lucy's chin came up, her violet blue eyes furious. 'You can walk away any time you like! OK?'

So the baby was a problem. Well, what other attitude had she expected from Joaquin? Few men would welcome being saddled with the consequences of a one-night stand! At least he was being honest, she tried to tell herself, seeking some saving grace in that blunt admission, but she still felt cut to the bone. She hadn't asked to be pregnant and she didn't want to be pregnant. In fact, right at that moment, the knowledge that there was a baby growing inside her just filled her with fright. She felt more like a teenager than the adult she had believed herself to be.

Joaquin closed long fingers over hers as she attempted to move away. 'We'll talk later,' he spelt out warningly, tightening his grip when Lucy engaged in a covert tug of war with his hand, and then disconcerting her entirely by using his other hand to separate her from the wine glass she was still holding. 'I'll get you a mineral water. I seem to recall that alcohol is not recommended, *es verdad*?'

'Will you just keep quiet about my condition?' Lucy hissed at him out of the corner of her mouth, seething emotions washing about inside her to such an extent that she believed she might explode from the pressure.

'My apologies,' Joaquin breathed with icy hauteur. 'But at this moment I can think of nothing else.'

Quelled by that confession, which was a most ironic match for her own troubled state of mind, they headed for the top table where a place had been made for Joaquin. As

she passed by her sister, Cindy broke off her conversation
with her father-in-law, rose from her seat with a beaming
smile and enfolded Lucy in a sudden effervescent hug.
'Congratulations, sis! Doesn't Joaquin move fast? I'm so
happy for you I could cry!'

A bewildered look stamped on her face as Cindy dropped
back into her seat, Lucy muttered, 'What on earth…?'

Joaquin urged her further down the table and into a chair.
'Naturally I informed Roger of my intentions.'

'What intentions? Roger?' Lucy questioned in a daze,
still struggling to work out what her twin had been con-
gratulating her on.

'*Dios mio*…he is your closest male relative. To whom
else would I have spoken?' His crystalline green eyes
veiled from her view by lush black lashes, Joaquin sank
with fluid grace down into the seat beside her. 'But never
before have I been so aware of the gap between your culture and mine. Had Roger been Guatemalan, he would not
have waited for me to approach him. He would have demanded the same result with a gun to my head and the
church already booked!'

'J-Joaquin…' Lucy whispered shakily, her throat closing
over as what he was saying began to make sense. But she
was hampered by the reality that she just couldn't credit
the 'result' he was talking about. 'Exactly what are you
saying?'

His beautiful mouth hardened. Tilting back his arrogant
dark head, he dealt her a cool, unimpressed glance that
questioned her apparent inability to follow his meaning.
'That we will be married just as soon as I can arrange it,
querida. What else?'

CHAPTER TEN

AT THE same instant, Roger stood up to make a speech.
But Lucy was welded to the formidable challenge in
Joaquin's cool gaze. Her mouth running dry, she tore her
shaken eyes defensively from his.

Strange how a proposal she would have received with
joy just a few days ago now filled her with a deep sense
of hurt and humiliation, Lucy conceded painfully. No wonder Roger and Joaquin had got so chummy so fast! But
what did Joaquin expect from *her*? Applause? Grovelling
gratitude? He had not even proposed to her! Although nothing had yet been discussed between them, although many
explanations had yet to be made on her part, Joaquin had
decided all on his own that there was only one solution.
An old-fashioned shotgun marriage with a bridegroom set
on doing what he felt he *ought* to do rather than what he
wanted to do!

Lucy thrust up her chin. 'With reference to the proposal
you put before my brother-in-law before you even thought
to mention it to me,' she countered tartly. 'No, thanks!'

At that point, Roger insisted on giving a toast to 'Cindy's
just-got-engaged-sister, Lucy.' Lucy shrank in her seat, face
flaming with self-consciousness and growing outrage. What
was wrong with everybody? Without one word of personal
assent from her, her relatives were happy to assume she
was getting married. Of course, it would certainly get her
out of their apartment. The minute she thought that silly
petty thought, she suppressed a groan and struggled to get
a rational grip on herself.

155

'Let's dance,' Joaquin suggested when the meal was at an end and the floor had filled.

'Forget it,' Lucy snapped, after maintaining the longest and most sullen silence in history.

'You're behaving like Yolanda!' Joaquin lowered his head to give her what felt like the ultimate put-down, brilliant green eyes exasperated.

Lucy reddened, stood up, and fought off an overwrought urge to both hit him and burst into tears. Joaquin tugged her into his arms. The achingly familiar scent of him enfolded her and did something crazy to her pulses and her heart. She closed her eyes, shaken to find that her wretched body was indifferent to her mental turmoil. The lure of that hard muscular physique against hers and the tantalising heat of him was almost impossible for her to fight. Little quivers of darting warmth glanced through her taut limbs, stirring up the hunger she would have done just about anything to stamp out. She trembled.

'"No thanks"?' Joaquin husked in effective repetition of her refusal an hour earlier, his silken derision sliding along her sensitive nerve-endings and then striking like a whip. 'If you were in my bed now you would give me a very different answer, *gatita*.'

At that crack, she stiffened, and missed a step. 'That's what you think—'

'That's what I *know*, for your desire for me is the only honest thing you ever gave me!' Joaquin breathed in a harsh undertone.

Lucy paled. 'All right... I should've told you the truth sooner—'

'You did not tell me the truth *at all*,' Joaquin slotted in with crushing precision.

'I was scared you would confront Cindy and cause more trouble between her and Roger before the wedding,' she argued feverishly.

'Poor little Lucy, always sacrificing her own best interests for those of others,' Joaquin countered with deeply sardonic bite. 'But isn't it remarkable that instead of becoming my mistress you will now become my wife?'

Her teeth gritting at that comeback, Lucy saw red. She stretched up on her toes to gasp into his ear, 'I wouldn't be your mistress if you *paid* me.'

'*Por Dios*...did you think I expected you to share my bed for nothing?' Joaquin enquired, smooth as glass. 'I cut my teeth on women considerably more calculating than you. I expected a price, but even I could never have dreamt that it would be a wedding ring!'

'Rot...in...Hades!' Lucy hissed the last word like a spitting cat and stalked off the floor to take refuge in the cloakroom.

That louse was the guy she thought she loved? She rinsed her hands under cooling water and shivered with angry confusion and a deep, deep sense of loss. Why was it she was now remembering his teasing warmth that morning he had called, before everything had gone catastrophically wrong? Though now she knew what the warmth had been angled at achieving, didn't she? Joaquin had still been planning to make her his occasional bed partner. So if she was in shock right now, so was he.

She clutched the edge of the vanity unit and breathed in deep on that latter acknowledgement.

Joaquin was still—quite understandably—seethingly angry with her. He might be putting on a show of cool for the sake of appearances, but just a couple of hours ago Joaquin had discovered that she had engaged in a really massive deception and that virtually everything he had believed he had known about her had related to her sister Cindy instead! Then Roger had seized probably the worst possible moment to persuade Joaquin into attending the reception. Why the heck had Joaquin agreed?

'Even if I wanted to, I'm not in a position to just walk away now,' Joaquin had said. So Joaquin had allowed Roger to smooth things over in the aftermath of all the bad feeling over Fidelio simply because Lucy was going to have his baby. But why had he immediately informed Roger that they were getting married? Relieved to see such a tidy conclusion to an impending drama, Roger had naturally been delighted to hear and share that news.

So what was she going to do? Stick her nose in the air and walk away just to show that she could do it? Or recognise that right now Joaquin had a perfect right to be furious at the games she had played in Guatemala? But had he really planned to make her his mistress? Recalling her visit to his London home, and the passion which would very probably have plunged her back into bed with him again, she flushed with embarrassment.

If making her his mistress had been Joaquin's ambition, he had been progressing well on that score. She might have found herself involved in a heartbreaking affair in which she was always waiting for his next phone call. Lucy spread thankful fingers across her still flat tummy. If there was a choice…and it was by no means certain that there *was* a choice—for she didn't want a reluctant bridegroom—she knew she loved Joaquin, and that she would rather be his wife than his mistress…

When she returned to the table, she saw Joaquin standing with Roger and Cindy. She watched his charismatic smile flash out, but noted that it didn't quite reach his eyes. For a male in the mood he was in, he was, however, putting on a heck of an impressive show. And why not? He was rich, he was sophisticated, he was the original Mr Cool on the surface…but underneath? He absolutely fascinated her. A secretive smile brought a dreamy curve to Lucy's mouth as she kept her distance and mingled with the other guests.

When it was time for Cindy to change so that she and

Roger could head for the airport, her sister took her up to the hotel room with her. 'So my former worst enemy is going to join the family...only you could have pulled that off in so short a time!'

'It's not quite as simple it sounds. I'm going to have a baby,' Lucy finally told her twin.

Cindy was dumbstruck. 'But of the two of us you're supposed to be the cautious, sensible one.'

'Human, too.'

'But you were only over there a few—'

'Long enough,' Lucy slotted in ruefully.

Cindy grinned. 'So I'm going to be an aunt and get to see what it's like being a mother before I try it for myself.' She hesitated, her face colouring. 'I guess Joaquin will bring you up to speed on the other business.'

Lucy frowned. 'What other business?'

'Never mind now. It's not something I want to think about any more,' Cindy gabbled in a rush, but she gave her twin a rueful glance. 'But I can tell you one thing... Joaquin's a really decent guy!'

On the way downstairs again, having refused to satisfy Lucy's curiosity as to what she had been talking about, Cindy paused to throw her bouquet. A crowd of young females gathered but Cindy threw her flowers wide and high and with deadly accuracy at Joaquin. 'I wanted *you* to have it,' she whispered to her twin.

Ten minutes later, the bridal couple having departed, Lucy climbed into Joaquin's Ferrari. 'I suppose we're about to talk,' she said tautly.

'Not a good idea while I'm endeavouring to hold on to my temper, *querida*,' Joaquin drawled in succinct warning.

'Feeling like that, it's just insane to talk about us getting married,' Lucy sighed.

'I don't see it in that light. I have a duty to my child *and* to my family name. There is no choice about how we handle this with my sixteen-year-old sister in the same household. We'll be married within three days.'

'Three days?' Lucy echoed in disbelief.

'If I cannot get a special licence for us to marry here within that time-frame, I will fly you back to Guatemala and have the deed done there.' His bold bronzed profile grim, Joaquin filtered his car somewhat aggressively into the traffic flow. 'The sooner we are married, the better. If I can contrive to shield my sister from the consequences of my own stupidity, I shall do so.'

Lucy hadn't thought of Yolanda, but now she did and she cringed with discomfiture. An out-of-wedlock pregnancy was not the way to impress a teenage sister with the principles which Joaquin would wish to instil.

'I...I could go away somewhere... I mean, obviously, I wouldn't keep in touch with her—'

'Don't be foolish. A child cannot be hidden for ever. Or perhaps you are thinking that the child should not be born. It is my wish that it should be!' Joaquin shot at her in a harsh but anxious undertone.

Lucy paled. 'It's my wish too.'

'*Por Dios*...then why are you arguing with me?'

She closed her aching eyes. Joaquin wasn't giving her a choice, but she still knew that she *had* a choice. Did she marry him because she loved him and she was carrying his child and hope that somehow, some way, they could work a miracle together? It could not be said that Joaquin was in a mood to be easily persuaded. It could not be said either that working miracles was on his mind.

'Why don't you just talk out how angry you are with me for pretending to be Cindy?' she muttered ruefully. 'I can take it...'

The silence just sizzled. He had so much emotion, but it was all under firm lock and key. He thought strictly in shades of black and white. She was pregnant. For him, that was a problem. He seemed to believe he could solve that problem as if it was any other everyday problem. He took no account whatsoever of emotions. Did he feel *anything* for her apart from anger?

Lucy surfaced from sleep and slowly pushed herself up on her elbows to find herself lying on a bed in an unfamiliar but decidedly masculine bedroom. The light by the bed gleamed over a silk tie lying across the arm of an antique chair. The last thing she recalled was being in Joaquin's car.

She checked her watch. It was almost midnight. As she sat up, the door opened and Joaquin entered. When he realised she was awake, he stilled and studied her with veiled eyes. Self-conscious beneath that scrutiny, Lucy pushed her tumbled caramel hair back from her face and tucked her feet beneath the white dress pooled around her.

'Your sister didn't choose that gown,' Joaquin commented. 'It's too elegant.'

Taken aback, Lucy coloured, but he was right. Cindy had stipulated the colour but her mother-in-law had chosen the style.

His penetrating gaze still glittering over her, Joaquin vented a roughened laugh. 'You look the very picture of Victorian innocence. In Guatemala, you wore only revealing clothes designed to attract male attention. Too short, too tight, too provocative.'

'Considering the way your own sister dresses—'

'But *only* in the privacy of her own home, in an effort to shock and annoy me,' Joaquin interposed wryly. 'I looked at you and I read the message in the clothes you wore.'

'What message?' Lucy was now taut, flushed and discomfited.

'That you were sexually available, that you knew the

score, that you wanted me to look and desire you,' Joaquin supplied with a raw edge to his dark deep drawl. 'I got the *wrong* message, *es verdad*?'

Lucy dropped her head, for there was a certain amount of truth in what he said. Cindy adored being the centre of male attention. Cindy always dressed on the edge of provocation. 'They weren't my clothes.'

'Did you think I hadn't worked that out yet?' Joaquin spread one lean brown hand in an angry movement. 'Just like you fondly imagined outside the church today that I might *not* be able to tell you and your twin apart?'

'A lot of people say they can't—'

'Then they're playing to the gallery. Cindy looks older. Same features, but different expression and cynical eyes.'

'I wouldn't have been too happy if you hadn't been able to tell us apart,' Lucy conceded.

'I would have been happier had I found out my mistake before you left my country,' Joaquin admitted, his beautiful mouth curling. 'I only ever intended to spend the one night with you—'

'Let's not talk about that,' Lucy cut in uncomfortably.

Joaquin dealt her a gleaming glance, his hard jawline squaring. 'I have never brought a woman to Hacienda De Oro. It is my family home. Out of respect for my female relatives I observe certain standards there, but desire overcame my fine principles,' he stated. 'I had nothing with which to protect you. I believed you had recently been living with a man—'

'I understand that.' Lucy just wished he would drop the subject.

'Do you? Precautions did cross my mind, but my hunger was stronger than my caution,'' Joaquin confessed curtly. 'So now we both pay the price.'

A wash of prickling tears hit the backs of her eyes. 'It doesn't have to be like that, Joaquin.'

'Do you think I'm whingeing like some teenage boy faced with his obligations?' Joaquin laughed with what sounded like genuine amusement, and that made her glance up in sharp disconcertion. 'Now that I have spent all afternoon and most of the evening counting the costs, let me count the benefits.'

'Benefits?' Lucy queried in surprise.

'I shall have you in my bed whenever I want. I shall have a child, and I like children. I will also get a keeper for my very troublesome sister.' As he spoke Joaquin closed the distance between the door and the bed and reached for her hands to pull her to him with easy strength. 'Yolanda's too old for a substitute mother figure, but just ripe for a big sister with a sympathetic manner. She likes you. You certainly made a hit there!'

Still trying to adjust to that volatile change of mood which had so taken her by surprise, she felt her mouth run dry as Joaquin just lifted her against him like a doll. Her heart hammered, the most wanton sense of anticipation rising as she collided with his shimmering green eyes. But Joaquin did not kiss her. Instead, he flipped open the door again, and she belatedly appreciated that he was actually taking her *out* of his bedroom.

'But maybe it's not Yolanda whom I most want and need to be a hit with...' Lucy confided in a sudden rush, the awkward sentence tripping off her tongue, ill-considered but honest in sentiment.

'It is all that is on offer, *querida*. Unlike you, I do not tell lies. If you did not have my baby inside you, you would not be here now.' Further down the well-lit corridor, Joaquin thrust open another door and carried her over to the bed.

'But I couldn't live with you feeling like that!' Lucy confessed, so great was her recoil from that blunt statement.

'I do not have one of those tolerant forgiving natures that

everybody is supposed to have these days,' Joaquin delivered in a driven undertone. 'I have a very strong sense of what is wrong and what is right, and what you did to me was *very* wrong. Do not ask or expect me to pretend otherwise.'

Having shattered her with that speech, he laid her down on the bed with careful, even gentle hands. '*Buenas noches*, Lucy.'

Lucy stared at the ceiling until her vision clouded with the strength of her stare. Tears trickled out of the corners of her eyes and stung her taut face. Well, she had asked how he really felt about her and he had told her. He had told her, with the kind of sincerity that scorched, exactly how he felt. She had been judged and found wanting and he did not believe that he would ever manage to forgive her. She couldn't possibly marry him. She couldn't possibly!

She tossed and turned all night, but eventually she weighed every possibility in the balance and that was when she decided that she *would* marry him. First and foremost their baby deserved that she made that commitment and try to make their marriage work. She would have to be patient where Joaquin was concerned, but with time and opportunity on her side mightn't he start seeing her in a different light? All right, so he didn't love her, but nobody got absolutely everything they wanted, did they? She was willing to compromise.

On the way downstairs next morning, Lucy could not help noticing the absence of any form of seasonal decoration, yet in little more than a week it would be Christmas day. Probably Joaquin and his sister always spent the Christmas period in Guatemala, she reflected.

Joaquin lowered his newspaper when she entered the dining-room for breakfast. Still clad in her bridesmaid's dress, because she had nothing else to wear, Lucy felt a little foolish.

'The special license will be granted for the day after tomorrow. I expect my diplomatic status helped.' Casting aside the newspaper, Joaquin rose to his full, formidable height, his well-cut charcoal-grey business suit accentuating his wide shoulders and lean muscular physique.

He took a lot for granted, and Lucy stiffened. 'I haven't said I'll marry you yet.'

Cool green eyes set in a darkly handsome lean male visage arrowed into hers. 'Will you?' he said drily.

Her colour heightened. 'Yes.'

'I never doubted it for a moment, *querida*,' Joaquin murmured silkily. 'One of my staff is handling the arrangements. The application requires a copy of your birth certificate.'

Anger and embarrassment claimed her and she bit down on her tongue before she said something she might regret.

'I suggest that you move in here today,' Joaquin continued evenly. 'Yolanda's school breaks up for the holidays tomorrow and she'll be home in the afternoon. I'd be obliged if you were in residence by then.'

Taking her seat at the beautifully set table, trying not to seem sensible of the attentions of the manservant pouring a cup of coffee for her, Lucy asked, 'Won't you be here?'

'I'll be in Paris by this afternoon.'

She worried at her lower lip. 'Tomorrow?'

'I'll be back in London late tomorrow night.'

As he headed for the door, Lucy scrambled up again. 'You're leaving now?'

'Tell me, am I likely to get forty questions *every* time I leave you?' Joaquin enquired drily.

Lucy reddened, but she nodded with unapologetic certainty.

His brilliant eyes shimmered over her face and then nar-

rowed. He caught one hand in her hair and pulled her
mouth under his in an onslaught that was so unexpected
that a tiny cry of surprise escaped her. It was a devouringly
hungry kiss that sent her reeling. The stabbing thrust of his
tongue sent a wave of excitement hurtling through to her
to the extent that his equally abrupt withdrawal felt like a
punishment.

Dark colour scoring his proud cheekbones, Joaquin re-
leased her and expelled his breath. 'I almost forgot. The
ring...'

Still recovering from that explosive kiss, Lucy watched
him lift a small jeweller's box from a side-table and extend
it to her. 'Ring?' she questioned, her heart starting to beat
even faster, her reddened mouth to curving into a smile.

'A betrothal ring.' Joaquin frowned, his beautiful mouth
harshly compressed as he made a positive production out
of glancing at his watch like a male severely pressed for
time. 'My sister will expect it. Take her shopping with you
for a wedding gown.'

'A wedding gown?' Lucy clutched the box in one hand
and made a speaking gesture with her other at what was
she actually wearing. 'But I could wear this—'

An expression of distaste crossed his lean strong face.
'No Del Castillo bride would wear a second-hand dress!'

He reached the door and then swung back to murmur
reflectively, 'Choose something white...a white dress. Full-
length and traditional.'

He was thinking of Cindy's bridal apparel, which had
been pink and short, she registered dully. 'Anything else?'
she asked, not really expecting a further response.

Joaquin contemplated the wall rather than her, hard jawline set in a stubborn thrust, apparently deep in thought
on a subject which she had not expected him to take one
iota of interest in. 'A veil...and perhaps a tiara...I'll have
my mother's jewellery flown over. You'll need a bou-

quet…white roses,' he stipulated without hesitation. 'And don't put your hair up.'

Lucy absorbed the surprising detail of his instructions with ever-widening eyes.

Joaquin sent her a slashing sidewise glance and his strong jawline set even harder. 'I'm thinking of the look of things for my extended family and friends…on film, you understand. We'll throw a big party and show the film at it when we return to Guatemala to see in the New Year.'

'So we'll be spending Christmas here?' Lucy gathered. 'May I order a tree?'

For the count of five seconds Joaquin looked as though he had not a clue what she was talking about.

'A Christmas tree…' she extended awkwardly.

'Do as you wish,' Joaquin said, with all the enthusiasm of Ebenezer Scrooge, his impatience palpable.

And then he was gone.

'The look of things'? For the sake of appearances alone? Lucy was very pale. She opened the jewellery box and caught her breath at the glittering diamond ring formed in the shape of a flower. It was exquisite and very unusual. An engagement ring, or as *he* had called it, a betrothal ring. 'My sister will expect it'. That stabbed her to the heart, and she couldn't help but think how painfully ironic it was that Joaquin should condemn her for the deception she had practised on him but then make it crystal-clear that he expected her to put on another dishonest charade where their marriage was concerned.

CHAPTER ELEVEN

'For a cheap dress that had to be bought off the peg, it looks really good,' Yolanda conceded forty-eight hours later as she appraised the wedding gown which Lucy wore from all angles.

'It was a very expensive buy!' Lucy protested.

'Lucy…you have a new scale of expense to learn now that you are about to become a Del Castillo. Anything that hasn't been specially designed for you is cheap!'

But it was *still* a dream of a dress. Alone, Lucy would never have entered the couture salon to which Yolanda had taken her only the day before. By that late stage, fretting at her failure to find anything which would be worthy of the tiara which Joaquin had mentioned, Lucy had been getting really desperate. The gown had been a sample, in a tiny size. Without a murmur about the inconvenience, it had been shortened to fit her last night and delivered first thing that morning, a delicate confection of rich fine fabric, its bodice and long slender sleeves overlaid with a very fine tracery of seed pearls.

'I think it is so cool that Joaquin just can't wait to marry you,' Yolanda confided with a grin, helping Lucy to anchor the magnificent diamond tiara to the lace veil. 'Yet when he followed us to London, whenever I mentioned you he changed the subject! I suppose that means that when a guy is really, really crazy about someone he doesn't want to talk about it like a woman does.'

'No,' Lucy agreed hurriedly, bowing her head.

She had not even seen Joaquin since he'd left for Paris. He had returned very late the previous night. With Yolanda in the house, determined that every tradition should be followed, Lucy had found her efforts to go down to breakfast blocked and had ended up eating off a tray instead, while being lectured on what bad luck it would be for her to see Joaquin before they met at the altar.

Following the ceremony, Yolanda was spending a few days with a schoolfriend. She and her brother had finally reached an agreement on her future. The teenager would board during the week but come home to the townhouse at weekends. After she had sat her exams in June, she would have the option of completing her education in Guatemala.

A limousine ferried Lucy and Yolanda to a little church on the outskirts of London. Lucy couldn't believe her eyes when she saw the equivalent of a whole camera crew in place, awaiting their arrival.

'This will make the television news at home,' Yolanda pointed out to her, surprised at Lucy's surprise.

In fact the whole ceremony was taped, but Lucy, who would have been very nervous about that idea had she known about it in advance, took account of nothing and nobody but Joaquin from the minute she walked down the aisle. And from the instant she entered the church his attention was on her. Joaquin was sheathed in a superb pale grey suit which threw into prominence his devastating dark good-looks. As his bright eyes met hers Lucy was conscious only of an intense sense of happiness, and every other concern just fell away.

The ceremony complete, the ring on her finger, Lucy floated back into the limousine on Joaquin's arm.

He gave her a slow smile. 'You look superb, *querida*.'

'Yolanda said it was a cheap dress.'

Joaquin laughed with rich amusement. 'The term is relative when used by my sister!'

'Oh, my goodness!' Lucy suddenly clamped a hand to her mouth in dismay. 'May I borrow your phone?'

'What's wrong?' he demanded, extending the carphone with a frown etched between his straight ebony brows.

'I was supposed to start work today and I totally forgot to ring and tell them that I wouldn't be taking the job after all!' While Joaquin looked on in apparent astonishment, Lucy called directory enquiries to get the number of the toy store and then rang to offer profuse apologies for not having informed them of her change of heart sooner.

'Why are you looking at me like that?' Lucy asked self-consciously when she had replaced the phone, her conscience at peace again.

'It *is* your wedding day. I'm amazed that you took the trouble to make that call.'

'I don't like letting people down.'

His lean strong features had hardened. 'Isn't it a shame that you couldn't afford me the same consideration?'

'If you're talking about me having pretended to be Cindy,' Lucy responded tautly, 'that is an entirely different matter.'

'*Por Dios*...you have a talent for understatement.'

Lucy breathed in deep. 'But I might have told the truth sooner had you not made so many unpleasant remarks about my sister's past and then gone on to suggest that her future husband ought to be warned about what she was like.'

'So that's your excuse. I was very angry about what the old man had had to suffer.'

'Cindy never intended *anybody* to suffer! She may have written stupid letters asking for money, but she honestly believed he could afford to be generous. That's not the same thing as being a con-artist.'

Joaquin shot her a darkling glance. 'Nor is it acceptable behaviour. And you do my image of *you* no favours in trying to imply otherwise.'

'I'm sorry. She's my sister and I love her...flaws in-

cluded,' Lucy stated, tilting her chin. 'People can change,
Joaquin. Finding happiness with Roger changed Cindy and
I didn't want to see her lose him.'

'*Infierno!*' Joaquin slashed back at her with a sudden
raging incredulity that wholly disconcerted her. It was
much as though she had thrown a match on a bale of hay:
the conflagration was instantaneous. 'Yet you had little concern for what I might think of *you!*'

'That's not true,' Lucy began shakily, paralysed to the
spot by the blaze of dark fury brightening his extraordinary
eyes.

'You let me call you a whore!' Joaquin condemned, off-
balancing her even further with that outraged reminder.
'You lied to me. Even the night we made love you were
still lying. But the worst, the most unforgivable of acts,
was to leave me believing that you were sleeping with another man and that you might not know whose baby you
were carrying!'

Lucy sat there like a little stone statue, heart thumping
in the region of her dry throat, motionless with sheer shock.

'I might have gone away...I might *never* have come
back. I might have abandoned you for ever. And did you
count the cost? Did you care? *No!*' Joaquin thundered in a
splintering crescendo of accusation, his lean strong face
rigid.

'I...I would have contacted you.'

'*How?* Do you think I would have taken your calls or
accepted your letters or even believed anything you said or
wrote?' Joaquin demanded with raw contempt. 'A woman
who let me believe such filth about her for longer than a
moment is not a woman I can be proud to have as a wife!
I can only hope you have more loving concern for our child
when it is born than you had for me!'

With that wrathful conclusion Joaquin sent the privacy
panel separating them from his chauffeur buzzing back and

rapped out something in Spanish. She soon knew what it was. The big limo came to an almost immediate halt and Joaquin thrust open the door and sprang out.

'Joaquin!' Lucy gasped. 'Where are you going?'

'I need some fresh air,' he gritted in a driven undertone, and closed the door on her again.

Fresh as opposed to the air she was polluting with her presence, she translated in a daze as the limousine pulled back into the traffic again. Joaquin vanished into the busy crowds of Christmas shoppers. She looked at her watch. They had been married for forty-five minutes. She blinked and slowly filled her lungs with oxygen again.

Suddenly she was faced with the acknowledgement that she had carelessly glossed over something huge as if it was no more than a molehill. Behind her the molehill had mushroomed into a volcano. She, who prided herself on her soft heart and her sensitivity, had behaved in the cruellest way imaginable, and as she sat there numbly attempting to justify herself she found that she could not.

There *was* no excuse for her having allowed Joaquin to spend two entire days believing that Roger was her lover, most particularly not when she was pregnant. Just because she had known it wasn't true; just because she had been afraid to come clean and admit who she really was there and then. She had hidden behind the defence that she *still* had to put Cindy first, but that was no defence at all. Yet she had tried to make Joaquin listen and he had refused to listen. He had been in such a temper she had let herself be rebuffed.

When she got back to the townhouse, she was too disturbed by the awareness of her own less than presentable behaviour to be embarrassed by the reality that she was alone. Joaquin was furious with her and she understood why. How could she have treated someone she loved as she had treated him? She knew how volatile he was.

Suppose he had just decided right then on the spur of the moment that even for the sake of their child he could not stand to be married to such a selfish, insensitive woman? Recognising what a state she was working herself up into, Lucy stopped pacing the floor and decided that she would be better occupied doing something with herself.

The twelve-foot tree which had been delivered the day before now stood in the hall waiting to be dressed. That evocative pine scent brought back hazy memories of Christmases when Lucy had been a young child. Before her parents had divorced they had always had a real tree, as opposed to an artificial one. Entering into the spirit of the occasion, Joaquin's urbane manservant had produced boxes and boxes of vintage decorations from the attic where they had lain almost twenty years, since Joaquin's mother's death. Apparently Joaquin and his late parents had once spent every Christmas in England.

Reluctant to remove her wedding dress, but determined to keep it clean, Lucy borrowed a large apron, donned it, and began to burrow into the boxes. Her enthusiasm increased with every box she opened, for she found beautiful handmade decorations which had more than stood the test of time. She was standing on a low set of steps fixing an exotic feathered bird to a branch of the tree when the front door opened two hours later and Joaquin reappeared, with a gaily wrapped parcel in his hand. She froze. Three feet into the hall, he froze too. He appeared transfixed by the sight of her.

'*Madre mia!*' Joaquin suddenly exclaimed, and setting aside the parcel in haste, he strode across the hall to close both arms round her. He lifted her down from the steps much as though he was reclaiming her from grievous danger on the edge of a cliff.

'Are you crazy?' he demanded tautly. 'The staff should be doing this.'

Lucy focused on his lean, dark devastatingly handsome face, a tide of sheer heady relief washing over her. 'I love dressing the tree—'

Joaquin elevated an ebony brow. 'On your wedding day?'

'I needed something to do.' Lucy snatched in a steadying breath. 'And before you say anything, I've got something to say. I wish I could give you some magical explanation of why I let you go that day Roger barged in without making you listen to me, but I *can't*! I think I had just got so used to pretending to be Cindy, to being passive on my own account—'

Joaquin reached out and linked his hands with hers in a feeling movement. His brilliant green eyes held hers. 'I can't stand passive.'

'Well, I swear that if you hadn't come to the church on Cindy's wedding day I would have come to you to explain!' Lucy broke in urgently. 'I was really upset that you should think those things of me.'

Joaquin was now gripping her trembling hands very tightly. Dulled colour marked his proud cheekbones. 'I shouldn't have abandoned you in the limo,' he conceded in a driven undertone. 'But I was afraid of what else I might say…the damage I would do.'

'But you were right. I didn't think of how you might have been feeling.'

'*Por Dios*…I felt like I was being ripped apart that day at your sister's apartment!' Joaquin admitted grittily. 'But the crowning nightmare was believing that you were marrying Roger. I came to the church intending to do whatever I had to do to prevent you marrying him but very much afraid that I would be too late.'

'And instead you found out that I wasn't even who you thought I was,' Lucy filled in, shamefaced. 'Joaquin, I'm so sorry—'

'No, your concern for your sister was understandable.' Poised very straight and tall, Joaquin lifted one wide shoulder in an eloquent shrug that dismissed his own previous anger. 'In the heat of the moment in Guatemala I *did* make a most dishonourable threat. How were you to know that I would never have carried it out? I am *not* the kind of man who would sink to the level of carrying disreputable stories about a woman to another man.'

Recognising the distaste stamped in his lean strong face, Lucy sighed. 'I should have known that too.'

His beautiful mouth compressed. 'How could you have? From the instant I laid eyes on you I was strongly attracted to you. That angered me, and in an effort to remind myself of who and what I believed you to be I made several offensive remarks. I cannot excuse myself for having said such things to a woman.'

'I was shocked,' Lucy recalled ruefully.

'*Sí*...I saw that too, and marvelled at it. Then, when you condemned my lack of courtesy, I was outraged—but you were right to reproach me.'

It was balm to Lucy's ragged nerves to learn that Joaquin had been strongly drawn to her from the moment he met her, and she looked up at him and gave him a rather tremulous smile, for the extent of her relief had brought her emotions very close to the surface. 'I'm just glad you're home now. I was scared you were halfway back to Guatemala!'

'I can be hot-headed, *gatita mia*,' Joaquin conceded, his full attention pinned to her lovely smiling face with an intensity that made her incredibly aware of his powerful masculinity. 'But I assure you that even in the grip of all my stubborn pride and fury, I could not be that big a fool!'

'I was worried...' Belatedly becoming aware of the ludicrous apron she was wearing, she tugged her hands from his, only to find herself looking in dismay at her grimy hands. 'My goodness, I need to wash…I seem to have got more dust on me than the duster!'

Turning away in some chagrin at how she must look clad in her silly apron and with her childishly grubby hands, Lucy started up the stairs.

'For causing you concern—I apologise…' Having tracked her up to the landing, Joaquin caught one of the hands she was keeping well away from her gown in his, to plant a kiss almost defiantly into the centre of her palm.

Her knees went wobbly as she collided in shock with his shimmering crystalline gaze. 'I love your eyes,' she heard herself mumble.

'So you told me many times when you were ill…' His wolfish grin flashed out with charismatic brilliance.

Dredging her attention from him again with the greatest of difficulty, Lucy sped down the bedroom corridor, only to find herself forestalled by Joaquin, saying very decisively when she headed for the guest room she had been using, 'Wrong door.'

Feeling ridiculously self-conscious over that reminder that they would now be sharing the same bedroom, Lucy hurried further down the passageway and across his bedroom, straight into the *en suite* bathroom to wash her hands.

'You are still so shy, *querida*,' Joaquin murmured with a rueful amusement that made her cheeks burn as he came to halt in the doorway. 'Only *now* do I recognise what a lousy actress you were in Guatemala. I told myself that the innocence I kept on sensing was a good act. I could not bear to want you so much and believe that you were out of reach. For of course, had I known the truth, it would have been dishonourable for me to take advantage of you.'

'You didn't do that.' Grabbing up a towel, Lucy hastily dried her hands.

'I *did*. Don't you know it's asking for trouble to go to bed with a man who tells you not to fantasise about a future? It was a line and you swallowed it,' Joaquin imparted in a seriously pained tone. 'You should have told me to get lost.'

'But I didn't want you to get lost,' Lucy answered truthfully.

'You were a virgin…'

Looking anywhere but at him, Lucy nodded her head in embarrassed confirmation.

Joaquin groaned out loud. 'All that nonsense you spouted to conceal that reality! I would have waited for our wedding night—'

'Joaquin…this is one of those subjects when cultivating a short memory would be the very nicest thing you could do for me.' Now frantically engaged in a struggle to untie the knot of the apron strings, so that she could shed the wretched garment and once more look like a normal bride, Lucy found herself receiving help. Joaquin edged her backwards out of the bathroom, spun her gently around and had her out of the apron in two seconds flat.

'The fault was mine. I was too proud to accept that I could be so much in love with a woman who seemed to be the total opposite of my every ideal,' Joaquin breathed ruefully.

'So much in love…?' That was all Lucy heard, and that confession just pinned her to the spot with a dry mouth and a madly racing heartbeat.

'Which is why I came to the church on your sister's wedding day. The minute I realised I might have lost you to another man, *nothing* else mattered!' Joaquin shared in a raw-edged admission. 'Not that you might have slept with him, not that the child might even be *his*…I still wanted you to be mine.'

'Oh, Joaquin,' Lucy muttered, her eyes glistening with helpless tears. 'I can't believe you loved me that much—'

'Didn't I rush to the church to tell you so?' A forgivably

grim smile of recollection momentarily curved his firm mouth. 'Only to discover that you were not Cindy Paez and not the bride either. Never have I been made to feel like such a fool! In anger with you, I almost let my pride destroy us then.'

Lucy touched his hand with uncertain fingers. 'You were allowed to be angry——'

'But I might have driven you away. I wanted to punish you for having deceived me. Yet, when I thought about it, I had always known the *real* you,' Joaquin stressed, spreading both hands in speaking emphasis on that point. 'The whole time you were just yourself in Guatemala. Honest in every way you could be. Very shocked to hear of Fidelio's situation, always attempting to show me that there were *two* sides to every argument——'

'You know...' Lucy broke in, so eager was she to share her own feelings at that moment. 'I love you very much too!'

Joaquin surveyed her with shimmering eyes full of appreciation, and his smile became one of unalloyed satisfaction, his brilliant gaze softening to tenderness. Nothing was said. In that instant nothing more *needed* to be said. He pulled her into his arms with unconcealed impatience and kissed her with the most explosive hunger he had ever shown her.

There was nothing remotely cool about the way in which he got her out of her wedding gown, nothing measured or smooth about the manner in which he stripped off his beautiful suit. They were both on an emotional high of sheer relief and happiness that all the misunderstandings were now behind them. From that first drugging kiss she was on fire, aching for the glorious fulfilment that only he could give.

In the aftermath of that wild passion, which swept them both to the heights and then dropped them down gently to share a wonderful sensation of togetherness, Luc[y] [recog]-nised that she had never felt so happy in her life. [T]h[at] sensation was made all the more intoxicating by the qui[et] awareness that Joaquin felt exactly the same way.

His bright gaze, semi-screened by his lush black lashes, smouldered over her with possessive intensity and then his mouth quirked. 'There's something I should tell you... I will personally replace the remainder of Fidelio's savings. He will never know that the money did not come from your sister.'

Lucy could not conceal her total disconcertion at that announcement.

Joaquin smiled ruefully and skated his fingertip over her full lower lip. 'Roger argued with me, but I insisted that clearing the debt would be my wedding present to them both.'

'But why...why did you change your mind and decide to do that?' Suddenly registering that this must be what her twin had referred to but refused to discuss before she'd set off on her honeymoon, Lucy was genuinely amazed that Joaquin had decided to make so generous a gesture towards her sister and her husband.

'I now believe that Fidelio and Cindy were *both* victims, in their own way. If Mario hadn't died, it would never have happened.' Joaquin sighed. 'But Mario was using my hotel suite when he met your sister. He was a very nice guy, but it is possible that in a desire to impress Cindy he somewhat exaggerated his circumstances and misled her entirely.'

Lucy nodded very slowly at this re-rendering of possible events. She had the tact not to comment. She saw that Joaquin had been realistically reappraising what he recalled of his former friend's character. A nice guy, but possibly not above the kind of boastfulness which might have come close to actual lying, she translated for herself.

'It is not a good idea for Roger and your sister to start

eir life as a couple with a substantial debt still hanging over them. They had already lost the value of that flat which was sold. Your sister is going to have a hard enough time living within their income,' Joaquin pointed out wryly. 'It occurred to me that to saddle them with so great a burden might put considerable strain on their relationship in the future.'

'Yes.' Lucy had been trying not to worry about that angle herself, but there was no denying that Roger would have had good reason for resentment when he found himself under such financial constraint. After all, he had not even known Cindy when the debt was incurred. Suddenly she was just filled to the brim with gratitude that Joaquin had had that much foresight and generosity.

'It means so little to me, but so much to them.'

'I just love you ten times more than I did a minute ago!'' Lucy told him exuberantly, for he was every bit as clever as she had ever thought he was.

Joaquin lay back against the pillows and let her cover him with kisses. He gave her a wry smile. 'Fidelio will also profit more from this less punitive way of resolving the situation. We will invite Roger and Cindy to Guatemala to meet the old man and that will make him very happy.'

'You're brilliant,' Lucy assured him, even more impressed and quite unable to hide the fact.

'I told you that you were made for me.' Joaquin studied her rapt face with tenderly amused eyes. 'The Latin male ego thrives on appreciation.'

Much later they ate by romantic candlelight in the dining room and Lucy unwrapped the gift which Joaquin had set aside and forgotten about when he returned earlier that afternoon. It was the most exquisite crystal angel.

'I saw it in a store. It made me think of you,' Joaquin confessed silkily.

'An angel?' Lucy queried a little tautly.

'Not quite,' Joaquin countered teasingly. 'But I can see through you the same way I could see through crystal.'

After their meal they finished decorating the Christmas tree, which had to be just about the very last thing Lucy had expected to share with a male of Joaquin's sophistication. But Joaquin, it turned out, was no more proof against the lure of happy childhood memories than she was, and he was drawn into the task the instant he recognised some of the vintage decorations which Lucy had already hung.

His mother, who had died when he was ten, had adored London. Christmas had never been the same after that for him. And Lucy had had much the same experience with her mother, after her parents had parted.

'It made me sort of crave all the festive trappings while I was growing up,' she confided ruefully. 'Mum just had no interest after my father walked out.'

'If you want to put a giant Santa Claus on the roof and cover the whole house in naff lights, you can, *gatita mia*,' Joaquin promised, appreciatively hugging her to him with all the affection and warmth she revelled in. 'Yolanda will come in the door and groan about how sentimental you are, but secretly love it all.'

Actually, he got that wrong. His sister came through the door on Christmas Eve, took one look at the gorgeous tree and gushed with unhidden excitement, 'Oh, wow, Lucy... you're going to do the whole *family* Christmas bit! Are we having a turkey for dinner, like British people do? Crackers to pull? Silly games? Do I get to hang a stocking? Open my pressies at midnight?'

'No, you'll have to be seriously cool and control yourself until dawn breaks on Christmas morning,' Joaquin delivered with gentle irony.

Yolanda gave him an amused look. 'Joaquin...I'm adult enough now to be in touch with my inner child.'

On Christmas Day Yolanda left a happy trail of wrapping paper right round the drawing-room, glorying in every gift right down to the cute and cuddly teddy bear in her stocking, and then went into seclusion with her phone to amuse herself talking to her friends.

'Next year will be our child's first Christmas,' Joaquin whispered huskily, banding his arms round Lucy, who was still dazedly studying the huge mound of gifts which had more than made up for all the disappointing Christmases in her past.

'Yes…' She sighed dreamily, thinking that the little inflatable Santa Claus which Yolanda had included as one of her jokey presents would no doubt be exactly what their child would like to poke and pummel.

'Not many women would appreciate a teenager around within a few days of their wedding.' Joaquin studied her contented face with deeply appreciative eyes. 'But you don't mind, do you?'

Lucy smiled. 'I like the feeling that I'm part of a family just as much as she does.'

He kissed her breathless, and her heart sang and her pulses raced. Sensible talk receded for some time, until Lucy recalled that they were supposed to be attending a church service before lunch. Aghast at how late it was, she leapt off the sofa with pink cheeks, shocked at herself. 'Joaquin…we nearly forgot about the service!'

Joaquin studied her with amusement and he laughed. 'Did we warn Yolanda that tradition is going to bite even deeper today than she appreciated?'

Upstairs, Yolanda groaned in mock suffering on her call to a friend. 'You have no idea how *soppy* they are—always holding hands like kids. And Joaquin is just *so* clueless it's painful to watch. He's given poor Lucy all these dreary, dreadful books on the Maya…and as if that wasn't enough to bore her to death, he's dragging her off on some ghastly mega-tour of ruins next month. As if what we've got at the foot of the garden isn't enough for him!'

'Yolanda!' Joaquin called.

A week before Christmas, almost a year later, Lucy settled her infant son into his bouncing cradle in the drawing room of the townhouse.

Cindy and Roger were coming for lunch in about an hour and a half. Lucy was wearing an elegant blue dress, purely and simply because Joaquin had remarked on how that shade matched her eyes. She smiled to herself now at the memory of how Joaquin had once described exactly how she should look at their wedding. She had been awfully dim not to immediately grasp that a guy who could even picture what flowers she should carry to the altar was a hopeless romantic and very much in love.

Jaime Enrique Del Castillo yawned to regain his mother's attention. He had black hair and blue eyes and he was the most peaceful laid-back baby ever. But then their first child had absolutely no reason to be anything other than happy and content, Lucy conceded with a grin. He was first and foremost the most important little person in the household, and he received an incredible amount of attention from his parents, his aunt Yolanda and the staff.

Having left school and gained reasonable results in her exams, Yolanda, now seventeen, was attending a London art college. She was showing some talent and was now more interested in becoming a famous artist than attaining fame as an It Girl. Lucy had had quite an input in that development and, having attained the greater freedom of being a student, Yolanda was growing up fast.

Lucy had experienced a truly blissful first year of marriage, and she could not have been happier. Soon after their wedding Joaquin had swept her off on a leisurely three-week exploration of the ruined cities of the Maya. Although visiting some of the less accessible sites had been ruled out by Joaquin, on the grounds that such exertion was unwise for a woman in the early stages of pregnancy, they had had the most fabulous time on that trip. Lucy was now learning about conservation methods and Joaquin was convinced he had found his soulmate. Yolanda had been known to remark that as company went her brother and Lucy could sometimes be a challenge, particularly when they got stuck into what she deemed 'that boring stuff'.

Cindy and Roger had visited Guatemala over Easter, and had been invited out to Fidelio's refurbished ranch. The old man had greeted Cindy with open arms, and Roger with equal warmth, counting them both as relatives and delighted that they should visit him. Fidelio Paez was every bit as sweet as Yolanda had once said he was, and, no longer hampered by her guilty conscience, Cindy had genuinely warmed to the older man.

Lucy and Joaquin's first child had been born late enough after his secret due date for the uncritical to assume he had been born only slightly early. Their blushes had been spared. Now, crouching down to watch her baby Jaime stare at the lights shimmering over the glittering ornaments on the Christmas tree with round, fascinated blue eyes, Lucy studied the beautiful eternity ring which she had received on her last birthday and decided that she was the luckiest and most spoilt woman in the world.

Joaquin strolled in, dark and devastating in a beige suit. He laughed as Jaime stretched out a tiny hand in the direction of a swinging bauble further out of his reach than he could yet calculate. 'He would swarm over that tree like a miniature demolition man if he could!'

'This time next year he'll be a trial,' Lucy forecast with fond anticipation.

Joaquin bent down and slotted a rattle into his infant son's empty hand. Jaime relaxed again. 'He'll be even more

entertaining than he is now. He's got a real tough-man grip
on that rattle…do you see that?'

Lucy nodded agreement and tried not to smile.

Joaquin straightened and snaked out a powerful arm to
catch her to him, brilliant green eyes scanning her amused
face. 'You're laughing at me again.'

'Jaime just doesn't look that tough to me yet,' she confided chokily. 'But I'll take your word for it. Both being
guys, I guess you have a special link.'

'*You*,' Joaquin filled in with hungry appreciative emphasis, claiming her parted lips with his own in the kind of
long, slow drugging kiss that always left Lucy reeling and
dizzy and which was very much a major feature of their
lives. 'A very, very special link. I adore you, *querida*.'

'*Sí*…' Lucy sighed dreamily.

'*Sí*…' Joaquin confirmed a little raggedly.

Jaime, who enjoyed a thoroughly undemanding itinerary,
and who had not the faintest notion of being a chaperon or
even being a tough guy at that moment, just went back to
sleep and left his parents in peace.

*An electric chemistry with a disturbingly
familiar stranger...
A reawakening of passions long forgotten...
And a compulsive desire to get to know
this stranger all over again!*

Because

What the memory has lost,
the body never forgets

In Harlequin Presents®
over the coming months look out for:

BACK IN THE MARRIAGE BED
by Penny Jordan
On sale September, #2129

SECRET SEDUCTION
by Susan Napier
On sale October, #2135

THE SICILIAN'S MISTRESS
by Lynne Graham
On sale November, #2139

Available wherever Harlequin books are sold.

HARLEQUIN
Duets™

**Don't miss
an exciting opportunity
to save on the purchase of
Harlequin and Silhouette books!**

Buy any two Harlequin or
Silhouette books and save
$10.00 off future Harlequin
and Silhouette purchases

OR

buy any three
Harlequin or Silhouette books
and save **$20.00 off** future
Harlequin and Silhouette purchases.

**Watch for details
coming in October 2000!**

PHQ400

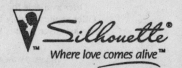